THE HORDE

THE
SPRIGGAN
BURROW

THE DEEP DARK

THE
HINKYPUNK
PATH

THE ODDMIRE

THE GOBLIN
PATH

SALAMANDER FLATS

ISLAND
OF BONES

ABBOT'S BAY

THE
ODDMIRE

BOOK THREE

DEEPEST, DARKEST

The Oddmire Series

Changeling

The Unready Queen

Deepest, Darkest

Other Books by William Ritter

Jackaby

Beastly Bones

Ghostly Echoes

The Dire King

THE
OĐĐMIRE

BOOK THREE

DEEPEST, DARKEST

written and illustrated by

William Ritter

Algonquin Young Readers   2021

Published by
Algonquin Young Readers
an imprint of Algonquin Books of Chapel Hill
Post Office Box 2225
Chapel Hill, North Carolina 27515-2225

a division of
Workman Publishing
225 Varick Street
New York, New York 10014

LIBRARY OF CONGRESS CATALOGING-IN-PUBLICATION DATA

Names: Ritter, William, 1984– author.
Title: Deepest, darkest / written and illustrated by William Ritter.
Description: First edition. | Chapel Hill, North Carolina :
Algonquin Young Readers, 2021. | Series: Oddmire ; book 3 |
Audience: Ages 8–12. | Audience: Grades 4–6. | Summary: Thirteen-year-old
twins Tinn and Cole, accompanied by friends and family, journey
beyond the heart of the Oddmire seeking their long-lost father.
Identifiers: LCCN 2020041304 | ISBN 9781643750927 (hardcover) |
ISBN 9781643751658 (ebook)
Subjects: CYAC: Adventure and adventurers—Fiction. | Twins—Fiction. |
Brothers—Fiction. | Missing persons—Fiction. | Magic—Fiction. | Fantasy.
Classification: LCC PZ7.R516 Dee 2021 | DDC [Fic]—dc23
LC record available at https://lccn.loc.gov/2020041304

10 9 8 7 6 5 4 3 2 1
First Edition

For my father,
Russ.

EARLIER

THE FOREST WHIPPED PAST THE THING IN A BLUR. It was feeling things it had not felt in a very long time—and some it had never felt at all. The pain, the cold, the fear . . . these were all too familiar. But nestled beside them now was something else, an exquisite ache. The Thing could scarcely breathe.

It had failed. It had tried to consume a changeling boy, and it had failed—and then everything had come crashing down. The boy's words echoed in its skull. *Nobody ever came for you, did they? That isn't fair.* The Thing burrowed its face into the soft earth, but that voice was everywhere.

His hand, gentle and warm, had scooped it up, held it close. The boy's eyes had looked down at it with such pity.

I am sorry that you suffered, the boy had said. *You didn't deserve that. You didn't deserve to be turned into this.*

The Thing dug more deeply now. It roared a furious roar to drown out the words and the feelings, but all that escaped into the cold night was a piteous wail, little more than the squeaking of a mouse. It was all too much.

It clutched at shadows, trying desperately to pull the darkness around itself as it once had, to create for itself an armor of icy midnight. The shadows melted through its fingers like smoke. Something had *changed*—not in the shadows, but within the Thing itself—and it couldn't put itself back the way it was.

The Thing did not want to be different. It burrowed deeper.

The Thing could still feel the warmth of the child's hands, clinging to it like tar. It had felt something else, too, while it was being held. It had felt—not anger . . . not hate . . .

The memory burned like acid in the pit of its stomach. Deeper and deeper it tunneled.

The Thing had felt . . .

. . . love.

But how? How could the boy treat it that way—after everything it had done, had tried to do, had *promised* to do? The boy had seen the Thing at its worst and he had not given up on it. He had greeted its sharpest barbs with tenderness.

Nobody had ever come for the Thing. The boy was right about that. The boy's family had come for him, and his friends, and even the forest folk. But *nobody* had *ever* come for the Thing. Not ever.

Except for the boy.

The boy had come for the Thing. He had knelt down and reached out for the Thing, held it, given it a chance. If, against every rational instinct, the boy could love a wretched creature such as it . . . then maybe the Thing was capable of being loved after all.

All at once, the ground beneath the Thing's fingers crumbled away, and it nearly dropped into a gaping underground cavern. The Thing caught itself and breathed in deeply. There were bodies moving below it in the dark; the Thing could sense them. It could also sense hopelessness and despair. The Thing closed its eyes and tasted currents of misery in the clammy air.

Yes. *This* was familiar. *This* was a flavor the Thing knew.

It drank deeply.

Around it, the darkness slowly thickened and coalesced once more.

Yes. This was right. Nothing had changed. The Thing could do great, terrible things down here.

ONE

"I'M GOING DOWN," SAID COLE.

"Watch your step," Tinn whispered.

The shaft was pitch-black and cold, and even the air felt heavy with the weight of the whole world pressing down on the twins. The yellow halo from the lantern bounced and bobbed as Cole eased himself down the stony slope, its light fading away a hundred feet or so into the fathomless dark. He held out a hand to brush the walls of the tunnel as he pressed forward. His feet shuttled as he slid down the path.

"It levels out again down here," he called up once he had found his footing. "Ow!"

"What happened? Are you okay?" Tinn skidded down after his brother. The crunch of his shoes and the skittering of loose pebbles resonated like an avalanche as they echoed all around him.

"I'm fine." Cole rubbed his head. "Watch the ceiling. It's low in here."

Tinn found his footing and put a hand on his brother's shoulder as they inched farther into the gloom. The flickering light danced across the broken handle of a pickax, abandoned against the tunnel wall. "That could have been his," whispered Cole. "Who knows how long this tunnel has been closed. He might have been the last person in here. We could be walking where he walked."

Tinn said nothing. He knew who Cole was talking about. It was all Cole wanted to talk about lately. Their father was more of a legend to the boys than a real person.

Joseph Burton had vanished nearly thirteen years earlier, when the twins were only babies. Popular rumor around Endsborough was that the man had run away because he knew one of his boys was a goblin in disguise. Old Jim had let slip that the last time they spoke, all those years ago, Joseph had been looking for a way to get rid of the imposter—to get rid of the changeling. Tinn's throat tightened. To get rid of *him*.

Tinn had known the story his whole life, but he had only

known *he* was the changeling for the past year. Knowing the truth cast a long shadow over Tinn's memories, and it twisted the thought of reuniting with the long-lost Joseph Burton into a complicated ball of feelings in his chest.

"I don't know if we should keep going," said Tinn. "They close tunnels like these for a reason."

"Just a little farther," said Cole.

"We'll be in huge trouble if Mom finds out we snuck down here."

"Who's gonna tell?" Cole answered. "If there's anybody working in the mines today, they're definitely not working in this one."

"Shh." Tinn put a finger to his lips. "You hear that?"

They both fell silent.

"Hear what?" whispered Cole.

Tinn closed his eyes, straining his ears for a few more seconds. "Nothing, I guess," he said at length. "I thought I heard footsteps or something tapping."

Cole shrugged. "It's called Echo Point for a reason."

He started forward again, watching his step and hunching low to avoid stalactites and rocky outcrops. Tinn followed suit.

"What if it's a knocker?" Tinn whispered. "We should really head back."

"What's a knocker?" asked Cole, still pressing forward.

"A Tommyknocker," said Tinn. "Evie has a whole page about them in her journal of creatures. She says all the miners know about knockers. They're spirits or ghosts who dress up like miners and hide in mines to cause trouble. Or sometimes they're nice, I think."

"Ow!" Cole lurched to a stop and rubbed his forehead with one hand. "Stupid tunnel."

"They say if you hear Tommy banging around in the caves ahead, there's going to be a collapse."

"That's just a superstition," said Cole. "She probably heard it from her uncle Jim."

"We heard about the Witch of the Wood from Old Jim, too," Tinn reminded him, "and we all thought *she* was just a superstition right up until we met her."

"That's different," said Cole.

"It's creepy down here. Let's go meet Evie and Fable like we said we were gonna."

"Just a little farther."

Tinn rubbed the back of his neck, but he kept up. "Kull told me a goblin legend about a group of explorers who dug too deep into the earth once," he said. "They got greedy looking for gold and gems and cut right into the heart of some sacred mountain. Instead of finding treasure, they unleashed a monster."

"You told me that one already," said Cole.

"No I didn't. I just learned it last week. You're thinking about the goblins who accidentally woke up a rock giant."

"Sorry. I can't keep it all in my head. You tell me a lot of goblin stuff."

"Actually, there's one more goblin thing I've been wanting to talk to you about—" Tinn began.

"Listen," said Cole, cutting him off. "I'm glad you like the stories. They're fun and all, but they're just not my thing. They're yours. I want to focus on finding Dad right now."

"Oh," said Tinn. "That's fine. I just thought you wanted me to tell you stuff I learn in lessons. I think it's neat that we get to know about this whole other world that we're a part of."

"*You're* a part of it," said Cole. "Not me. The goblins have made that very clear. I can't set foot in the horde without getting a spear pointed at my nose. Watch your step, there's a dip there."

"You're still a part of it. That's just the old-fashioned goblins, and they'll come around eventually. Kull and Chief Nudd aren't like that."

Cole chuckled. "Kull would probably be just as happy to make a stew out of me if he didn't know it would make you mad."

"Kull's not like that. He looked out for us from the shadows—both of us—for our whole lives."

"Sure, that's fair. It's super creepy, but it's fair. C'mon. I know Kull cares about you, and he's basically like your goblin dad. Nobody's taking that away—but our *real* dad is still out there."

"Kull is *real*," said Tinn. "He's more *real* than a stupid picture on a fireplace."

Cole glanced back over his shoulder with a scowl. "I don't get it. We spent all these years wondering what happened to him, and now that we finally might have a chance to find our actual dad, why are you acting all *weird*?"

"Because he's *not* my actual dad!" Tinn hadn't meant to raise his voice. He hadn't meant to say it out loud at all, but he had been thinking it for weeks, and now he found it tumbling out of his mouth before he could stop it.

"Oh, shut up." Cole rolled his eyes and turned to trudge deeper into the tunnel. "Of course he's your dad. Just because you came from somewhere else—you should know better than anyone that family isn't just about blood."

"It's *not* about blood. You don't get it. Maybe he was *your* dad before he left, and maybe he loved *you* and cared about *you*—but the only relationship that man ever had with me was trying to figure out how to get *rid* of me."

"That's not—" Cole began.

"It's true." Tinn stopped walking, and after a few paces, Cole turned to look at him. "I'll always be your brother—and

I'm not backing out of finding him. I want to help you see your dad again, I really do. But when we do . . . I just . . . I just don't know where I'm gonna fit into it."

"With me. With us. A part of it. Like always. Nothing has to change."

Tinn sighed. "Right," he said, unconvincingly.

"Looks like we'll be heading back after all." Cole held the lantern up. The tunnel's ceiling slanted gradually downward for about ten more feet and then ended abruptly when it met a wall of craggy rocks. "Another dead end."

"Good," said Tinn. "Let's go home."

"Wait. Hold on just a second." Cole lowered the lantern. He tapped the floor ahead of him with his boot. It clunked.

"Boards?" said Tinn.

Cole looked up, and the lamplight glinted wild in his eyes. "They're covering a gap in the rocks. I can feel air, too," he said. "I bet there's another shaft or a cavern or something right below us."

Tinn knelt next to him and brushed dust from the ancient wood.

"It's hard to get a good angle," said Cole. He clambered out onto the boards, turning the lantern this way and that. He hunkered down on his hands and knees, prying at the beams.

"Be quiet a second," said Tinn. "There it is again! I think it's getting louder. You can't hear that?"

Cole raised his head. "I don't hear anyth—"

But a noise cut him off. It was a creaking, groaning sound that tapered off into tapping, like the settling of an old house on a cold night. It was impossible to gauge where it came from—the noise echoed through the narrow tunnel, chasing and doubling over itself until it gradually faded away.

Tinn didn't breathe for several seconds. "Ghost?" he whispered.

"That's no ghost," said Cole at last. "That's just the sound old wood makes when it's straining."

Tinn glanced down. "You mean like old wooden planks with a couple of kids climbing all over them?"

Cole hesitated. He shifted his weight. The timbers beneath his knees groaned loudly. He gulped. "Sorta like that."

And then there was a crack.

"Move!" yelled Tinn. "Get off it!"

The platform splintered.

The board under Cole's right knee went first, and as he tried to catch himself, the one under his left snapped, too. His legs kicked as they found themselves suddenly hanging over empty air.

Cole dropped the lantern, clutching with both hands for a hold that wouldn't give way. The light clattered against the crumbling wood and then slid down through a crack into heavy darkness. It fell for a long time before it struck the ground with the distant crunch of breaking glass. The flare of the oil catching fire all at once painted the shaft in golden light, illuminating Cole's terrified face from below.

"I'm slipping!" Cole gasped.

Tinn planted his feet at the edge of the gap and grabbed Cole's hand just as the whole platform sagged. Cole clung to his brother with both hands as bits of broken boards clattered against the side of the shaft, tumbling twenty, fifty, a hundred feet down to land with distant bangs against the rocky floor.

Cole's fingers tightened. "Don't let go!" he cried.

Tinn could feel himself losing the tug-of-war as, against his desperate efforts to fight it, his brother's weight tipped him slowly forward.

Tinn's stomach felt strange. Time slowed. The world seemed clearer somehow, as if light were flooding the darkness of the tunnel around them. And then, just as Tinn felt his weight shift past the final tipping point—moments before he and his brother plummeted down the rocky shaft—a hand grabbed his shirt collar from behind and jerked him back to solid ground.

He felt his brother's hand ripped away, but the dusty figure caught Cole's arm as well. With another heave, they were safely free of the pit, panting and rubbing their bruises.

The boys turned their eyes to their rescuer. He wore faded coveralls and a dust-brown coat. On his head was clipped a lantern, which swiveled from one boy to the other. They squinted into the bright light.

"Thank you for saving us," panted Tinn.

"Dang," the figure grunted. "You look just like him." His voice was deep and dry.

"Sir?" said Cole.

"Reckless like him, too," the man said.

"We look like who?" asked Cole.

"Like the last fool I had to pull outta this mine shaft. Yer old man, if I'm not very much mistaken."

The figure tipped his helmet up so that the light flooded the ceiling instead of their eyes, and at last the boys could see the face of their savior. Peppery stubble swept the man's chin and hard wrinkles creased his forehead, but his eyes were soft.

"You *are* Joseph Burton's boys, I presume?" the man said.

Cole's breath caught in his throat. "You knew our dad?" he managed.

The man nodded solemnly. "Might be the last person ever saw him alive, sad to say."

Cole's mouth opened, but no words came out.

The tunnel was quiet except for the muffled sputtering of the lamp and the faint crackle of flames in the distance. The fires below had begun to consume the fallen boards, and in the faint orange glow, shadows fluttered like phantoms on the ceiling above the hole.

"Could we maybe talk somewhere else?" suggested Tinn. "Somewhere a little less horrifying and life-threatening?"

TWO

Fable swung gently back and forth in a hammock of vines. It was a good day. Evie Warner had finally gotten permission to spend an afternoon exploring the Wild Wood, and Fable had been doing her best to show Evie *everything* before it was time for her to go home. Evie hung on Fable's every word, writing furiously in her notebook with a fancy new fountain pen her mother had sent her from the city.

Already the two of them had skipped across the salamander flats and rustled brownie thistles, and Fable had told Evie which of the shiny violet berries were tasty snacks and which ones made you barf sparkles. Evie could not have wished for a better guide. Fable had been raised in this forest. Her mother was the infamous Queen of the Deep Dark and resident Witch of the Wild Wood—and the forest had begun to accept Fable as the heir to that magical mantle. Fable could have crossed every hill and valley of the Wild Wood with her eyes closed.

"Do you think we'll see any trolls today?" Evie asked. "Or nymphs? Cole told me you know one who can tell the future."

"Kallra? She's more of a water spirit," said Fable. "And mostly she just swims around and turns into frogs and stuff."

"Is that a spriggan?" Evie peeked into the underbrush. "Hello, there!"

"It's probably not a spriggan," said Fable. "You almost never see spriggans unless they want to be seen. I don't think anybody's spotted them around since the big battle at the Grandmother Tree."

"We have been attending to our own concerns," rasped a voice from the bushes.

Fable nearly tumbled out of the hammock. "Whoa. You *are* a spriggan."

"We are," said the voice. The figure who emerged from the brush barely came up to Evie's ankle, and its whole body was armored in something that looked like rough tree bark with a dusting of lichen. The girls both knew well enough not to let its appearance deceive them—spriggans were one of the most notoriously dangerous factions in the whole forest. "And you are correct. You are seeing us now because we wish to be seen. Scouts informed us of your location in the wood, and we were sent directly from the Oddmire Burrow to request an audience."

"Oh, jeez," said Fable. "I know a lot of forest folk have been calling me Little Queen, but my mom's still the one you want to talk to about official stuff."

"We do not wish to speak to your mother. We do not wish to speak to *you*, either," rasped the spriggan. "But you may remain, if you like, while we discuss matters with the human emissary."

Fable turned to Evie.

Evie's eyes widened. "*Me?*"

"You were the first to broker peace on behalf of your people," the spriggan said. "When the forest folk and humans clashed, you demonstrated courage on the battle-field and aided our nest in the retrieval of irreplaceable, sacred artifacts—all in spite of great disrespect shown to you by our kind."

"You *did* try to kill her," Fable added, helpfully.

"As I said—*disrespect*," answered the spriggan.

"I was just trying to put things right," said Evie. "I'm nobody special. I'm not an emissary."

18

"By the traditions of the nest—you *are*," said the sprig-gan. "The merits of your deeds have been weighed and considered. A ruling has been made. We are most displeased to find ourselves indebted to you. This is unacceptable. You are therefore to receive a requital immediately."

"I . . . don't even know what that is," said Evie.

"I think you're getting a reward," said Fable. "How come *I* didn't get a reward? I'm the one who caught the bad guy."

"The merits of *your* deeds were measured and found . . . balanced." The spriggan glared at Fable. "*Barely.* The nest does not currently wish you harm—but we have not forgot-ten the pudding incident at the Western Burrow."

"Pssh. Fine." Fable crossed her arms. "So what does Evie get?"

"I really don't need any reward," said Evie.

"You refuse our offering?" the spriggan said. "Such a blunt discourtesy will be met as a declaration of contempt and treated as an act of war."

"No, no! I would very much like to accept your gift."

"Good."

The spriggan chirruped and made a motion with one hand, and three more spriggans materialized from the bushes. The one in the middle was holding a bottle no bigger than one of Evie's fingernails. Within it swirled a purple liquid.

"What is it?" asked Evie.

"It has been observed," said the spriggan, "that the emissary wishes to learn about the many creatures who dwell in the Wild Wood. It has also been observed that, unlike most humans, she is possessed of a rare integrity to do so without intent to do harm."

"Yeah," said Evie. "That's true."

"We also value knowledge. We watch. We learn. We speak the tongues of over a thousand beings. On the rare occasion when we encounter a beast with whom we cannot communicate, we employ the Elixir of Melampus. One drop on the tongue grants the drinker the temporary ability to use and understand the language of any sentient being or savage beast. It will *not* give you power over them—you will *not* command them to follow your will—it will merely grant you a few moments of communication so that you might learn from each other."

"Y-you're giving me . . . my very own magic ability to talk to animals?" Evie stammered. "You mean it? For real?"

"You are being allotted a single draft—enough to employ its power one time and one time only. In my lifetime, the Elixir of Melampus has never been shared outside the nest. Do not take this offering for granted."

"I won't! I promise! I'll keep it super safe."

Satisfied, the spriggan nodded, and the other three

trotted forward and held up the tiny bottle. Evie took the elixir as if it were a precious snowflake that might melt away at any moment.

"Thank you," she whispered, but by the time she looked up, the spriggans had already vanished into the trees.

"Well, *that's* neat!" said Fable, coming to peek at the bottle. "Too bad it's just one dose."

Evie looked like she might cry. "Is it real, do you think? It's real magic?"

"Duh. Spriggans can be jerks, but they never lie," said Fable. "What do you think you'll use it on? I'd ask a dog why they like to sleep with their noses in their butts."

Evie just stared at the swirling purple liquid. "I . . . I don't know. I'll have to save it. It has to be for something really special. What does it feel like?" She tore her eyes off of the bottle long enough to turn them, sparkling with wonder, to Fable. "When you do magic?"

"What kind of magic?" Fable said.

"Any magic. Do different magics feel different? I bet it feels awesome."

"I guess." Fable had never given it much thought. She had been doing magic of one sort or another her whole life. Her mother was the Witch of the Wood, so magic lessons had been delivered with no more pomp than math or reading. "I don't really think about how magic *feels*. I just do it."

She considered for a moment. "Slappy sparks feels kinda hot. Oh, and when I compel vines I get a sort of lifty-uppy feeling behind my ears."

"That's so neat."

"Isn't it?" Fable smiled broadly and swung a little wider in her vine hammock. It was a good vine hammock. Probably her best one yet.

"Can you speak any other languages?" said Evie. "Like Pixie or Gnomish or anything?"

"Just the common tongue, but everyone speaks a little of that," said Fable. "Plus I can do people words. And bear. Being able to understand any animal would be pretty handy, though. You've got yourself an honest-to-goodness magic power that even I can't do. There was a while when my mama tried teaching me how to say *I'm sorry* in as many dialects as possible, but it never seemed to stick. Gnomes mostly talk human words anyway, so they're easy."

"Are they good guys?"

"The gnomes?"

"Yeah. Uncle Jim says gnomes are mischievous and like to cause trouble—but he says that about pretty much everything that lives in the Wild Wood. And about most kids. And a few adults. Mrs. Grouse says gnomes are good, actually. She says they do things for people sometimes, like fixing fences and stuff."

"I don't know what *all* gnomes are like—but I've met Bram Hobblebrooke a buncha times. He's a gnome. He gave my mom rare flowers once."

"That's sweet."

"Yeah. They were poison flowers."

"Wait. What?"

"Poison flowers. You know. The kind that moms like to smoosh up and keep in little black jars. So Mr. Hobblebrooke is okay, I guess. If you were drowning in the mire he probably wouldn't jump in to save you, but he wouldn't throw rocks at you either. He might poke a stick at you."

"To rescue you?" Evie asked. "Or just to poke you?"

"Definitely one of those reasons," said Fable. She shrugged. "Gnomes do get treated kinda crummy sometimes by the other forest folk. I don't know why."

"Maybe because they're small?" suggested Evie. At twelve years old, Evie was still just under four feet tall, even when she wore her thickest boots and stood up her straightest. She knew better than most how many people liked to pick on someone just for being little.

"Maybe," said Fable. "But there's lots of forest folk much smaller than gnomes. Sometimes I think folks just pick on other folks because they want to feel like they're better than somebody."

"Being a worse person is a pretty stupid way to make yourself feel like you're a better person," said Evie.

The ground beneath Evie's feet suddenly shuddered, and a cloud of finches took flight from the bushes behind her. Fable sat up as her hammock rocked. Evie's lips moved silently as she counted the seconds. Slowly, the rumbling eased and died away.

"Almost thirty seconds that time," Evie said when the earth was still again.

Fable scowled. "Mama says not to worry about the quakes," she said.

A frightened screech pierced the calm of the forest. Evie spun around, and Fable flipped out of her hammock and landed beside her in a tense crouch.

"What is that?" Evie whispered, but Fable was already racing into the brush toward the source of the noise.

The Wild Wood bent to Fable's will as she ran, branches bending out of the way and knotty roots flattening to form an even path. Evie took a deep breath and hurried after her. She kept up as best she could, but found the forest much less hospitable to her.

When she emerged from a patch of ferns into a slim clearing, Evie froze. The landscape was all wrong. A broad maple had tipped nearly sideways ahead of her and was slipping by slow degrees into a great gaping hole in the forest floor. Evie blinked. A thick clump of grassy sod broke free and tumbled into a widening gap. All around it, the earth sloped down toward the rift, like the dip in a sink before the drain. Evie took an involuntary step backward as she caught her breath.

Fable stood at the edge of the sinkhole. Her fists were clenched and her arms were shaking with effort. Evie watched in awe as, ever so slowly, the maple began to right itself. One thick, curly root rose up out of the chasm, and there—clinging to it for dear life—was a terrified opossum. The creature squealed pitifully as it slipped.

Fable only had one chance to get the timing right. She released her mental hold on the tree and put all of her energy into whipping a bright green vine across the gap. She could do this. She could catch the terrified creature out of the air and pull it back to safety. The opossum fell. The vine whipped.

Fable missed.

The opossum's squeal of fear hit Fable's stomach like a lump of ice. And then, abruptly, the squeal became a squeak of surprise. The ground beneath Fable slithered as every plant around the gaping hole came to life.

For just a moment, Fable had the giddy, nervous thought that this was her, that she was controlling things without even realizing it. It would not be the first time. But then she raised her eyes and saw her mother, her bearskin hood thrown back and her hands outstretched.

A much sturdier root than the one Fable had grabbed was now sliding upward, lifting the petrified opossum out of the pit. The queen's arm bent gently to the left, and the root echoed her motion, depositing the shaking creature safely on solid ground. It squeaked once more and then scampered away, vanishing into the brush. Raina did not break concentration. More glistening roots stretched across the yawning gap, darting with liquid grace like long snakes, coiling and uncoiling as they moved under her silent instruction. On either side of the hole, they pierced the earth like tent spikes, knitting a crude web over the opening.

Fable shook out her hands and joined the effort, lacing fine grasses and thick moss over the patch of vines to fortify the bond as they slowed and stiffened. When, at last, her mother let her arms fall to her sides, Fable flopped down onto her back in the moss to catch her breath.

Raina, Queen of the Deep Dark, stepped into her line of vision, looming over Fable's head.

"Hi, Mom."

"What did you learn?" Raina asked.

Fable took several slow breaths before answering. "The earthquakes *are* getting worse," she said. "The forest is breaking."

"Why did you stop?"

"What?"

"Why did you cease your efforts when the animal fell?"

"I—I couldn't do it."

"Wrong."

"I missed. I failed."

"Wrong. What do they call you, all across the forest?"

"Little Queen?" Fable mumbled.

"Correct. You *are* a queen." Her mother's voice was unyielding. "And there is no such thing as *too late* for a queen. There is only *now*, and *now* belongs to a queen. Fail, Little Queen. Fail a thousand times, but remember that as soon as you have failed, that failure belongs to *the past*. It is no longer your concern. A queen learns from the past and makes her next move swiftly and decisively."

Fable nodded meekly.

"So. Tell me what you learned."

"No such thing as *too late* for a queen," Fable grumbled.

Raina gave a curt nod of approval and turned to go. "You still have chores to finish. Don't forget to detangle the witching knots before sundown."

After the queen had gone, Evie finally crept forward. Fable was still lying on her back staring up at the treetops.

"Are you okay?" Evie asked.

"Yeah." Fable pushed herself up. "Come on. It's your

big day out. Let's go poke the Oddmire with sticks or something." She shot Evie a smile, but underneath she looked as if the whole forest was slowly coming to rest on her shoulders.

Evie nodded and followed as Fable led the way.

"I could've talked to that opossum," said Evie, quietly, just to herself, "if I wanted to."

THREE

"Winston," the man said as Cole and Tinn followed him out of the darkness and up to the mouth of the tunnel. "Winston Bell."

"I'm Tinn," said Tinn. "And he's Cole."

"Tinn and Cole." Bell nodded, smiling. "Of course you are."

"So, you worked with our dad?" asked Cole.

"I did." The man ducked under the weathered boards that blocked entry to the unstable shaft and stepped out into the open air. "Showed Joseph the ropes during his first weeks." He pulled off his helmet and snuffed out the lantern attached to the front of it. His hair was peppery gray and thinner on the top than the sides. "He and your mama had only just moved in. Sweet young couple. Annie was still pregnant with you." He hesitated. "Well, *one* of you, I suppose."

Tinn's eyes watched the ground. "With Cole," he said, quietly. "I came later."

"Sure did, didn't you," said Winston. "Caused quite the stir. Came to see for myself a few days after you showed up. Half the town paraded through your poor folks' cottage at some point that week. Word gets around quick in a town like this. Don't expect you remember any of that, though."

Cole shook his head. Their mother never liked to talk about those messy, hectic days right before Joseph had gone missing.

Tinn said nothing.

Mr. Bell slowed, eyeing Tinn's expression. "People didn't know what to think, back then. Didn't know who you were gonna turn out to be."

They crossed the dusty field toward the Echo Point base, a humble, weathered building with a tin roof and dirty windows. The air was still crisp, but the sun felt warm on their cheeks as they walked. The boys could hear the slosh of water and the murmur of voices. A hundred paces away, a handful of men shuffled around a long wooden sluice. A water wheel turned lazily beside it.

"It's funny," said Bell. "When he first started, Joseph was the last person to believe any of our old stories about goblins and the like. Miners can be superstitious folks. More than a few of us swear we've seen a blue-cap at the end of a tunnel or spotted the Lady of the Mountain out of the corner of one eye. Joseph thought that was all a bunch of nonsense. Well . . . until you came around. Took a pretty keen interest in stories then. He swore he heard voices in the old tunnels and asked me what I knew about kobolds and witches."

Mr. Bell slipped inside the base and emerged with a dented metal lunch box. It was bright red and had the initials W.B. inscribed on the lid. He sat down on the steps and patted the wood for the boys to join him.

"Did he talk to you about it?" Cole said. "About us? About what he was feeling before he . . . before he left?"

Bell shrugged. He plucked an apple from the lunch box and began slicing it with his penknife. "Yes and no. Didn't talk about feelings much, but you could tell he was all sorts of distracted. I remember I gave him grief more than once on that last day for getting in the way of the wagoners."

He passed a slice of apple to Cole.

"Think fast," said Cole and tossed the slice to Tinn.

Tinn wasn't looking, and the apple landed in the dirt.

"He was trying to figure out how to get rid of *me*," Tinn said. "*That's* what was on his mind."

Bell sighed and frowned. "He didn't know any better, kid."

The three of them sat in silence for a long moment while the water burbled gently in the background. One of the other miners out by the sluice said something too quiet to overhear, and another chuckled.

"He would be right proud of you today, though," Bell said. "You're his spittin' image, you know."

Tinn shook his head, scowling into the dirt. "I don't look like him."

"Sure you do. Heck, put a smudge of coal dust on your cheeks and a helmet on your head, and I would think your old man was back here sitting in front of me."

"That's Cole. *Cole* looks like our dad. I just look like Cole."

"Stop it," said Cole. "You're being dumb."

"I'm being honest," said Tinn. In a blurry wave, his skin was suddenly green and splotchy. Pointed ears rose out from his messy hair, and between his lips poked a row of sharp teeth. "*This* is what Joseph was worried about."

The sound of laughter in the distance halted. Tinn could feel half a dozen faces turning to look. He transformed back, but it was too late. Silence hung heavily over

Echo Point. Tinn's chest tightened and he put his head on his knees, wishing he hadn't been so stupid.

"If he *had* known what you are," said Cole, "what you *really* are—deep down—he wouldn't have been worried at all."

Tinn did not respond.

He heard the shuffle of movement and opened one eye to see Winston Bell standing up. "Come inside," the man said. "There's something you need to see." Bell stumped into the base without waiting for a response.

Tinn lifted his head. Cole shrugged at him, and the two of them pushed themselves up and followed.

The interior of the building smelled like firewood and clay dust. There were rugs on the floor and a brick fireplace at the far end with one thick log burning away. On one end of the room was a simple kitchen space with coffee mugs hanging from pegs over a washbasin. On the other end stood rows of lockers. Bell tucked his bright red lunch box into one of these and closed it with a click. On the wall beside them hung a huge framed map of the mining operation. Next to it were tacked two faded pieces of paper. One of them said *Safety* and held a list of rules. The other paper had come unpinned at the top and curled down over itself.

It was to this paper that Bell turned next.

"You boys used to be *Thomas*," he said. "Before you were Tinn and Cole, you were both Thomas. Did you know that?"

They nodded. Thomas Burton was the name on their birth certificate—the only birth certificate they had between the two of them. It was the name given to them back when there had only been one of them. Obviously the boys couldn't share a name forever, so some choices had been made.

"Your mama ever tell you where your new names came from?"

Tinn looked at Cole. Cole shrugged. "It was just a mining thing, I guess," he said. "A play on words."

Mr. Bell reached out a hand and smoothed the curling paper so they could read it.

"Is that a . . . poem?" said Cole.

"Mm." Bell nodded. "The owner put it up here ages ago."

He plucked a few spare tacks from the corner of the map and stabbed them into the top of the faded page to hold it up properly.

"Caught your old man copying it down on a piece of paper once, right at the end of our shift. Everybody was headed home, and he was in here, scribbling away. I asked him what he was doing that for. Wanna know what he told me?"

The boys nodded.

"He told me: *I don't know any lullabies. Working on learning one.*"

Bell stepped back and let the boys get a good look at the page hanging on the wall. The poem read:

> *More precious than the purest gold*
> *are humble brothers, tin and coal.*
> *They are not rich, but compensate*
> *by making those around them great.*
>
> *No matter how a diamond gleams*
> *it cannot give an engine steam,*
> *or save the strongest steel we trust*
> *from falling prey to age and rust.*
>
> *Supportive and dependable*
> *are far more recommendable.*
> *So be not swayed by gloss and shine*
> *when choosing what you want to mine.*
>
> *Seek out the seams that fortify*
> *and keep you sturdy, warm, and dry.*
> *More precious than the purest gold*
> *are humble brothers, tin and coal.*

Cole read the poem twice.

"Kept that paper folded up in his pocket the rest of the week," said Bell. "He'd take it out from time to time and I'd see his lips moving as he read. He was reading it the last time I saw him. I told him to get some rest. He stuffed it away, grabbed his lunch box, and headed out like normal. Except that was it."

"What do you mean, *that was it?*" said Cole.

"That was the last night. He never made it home. Nobody ever saw him again after that."

Tinn looked at Cole. Cole's eyes glistened in the light of the flickering fire, unblinking. He was still staring at the poem.

"The last thing on Dad's mind before he vanished," Tinn said, "was a lullaby?"

"For brothers," said Cole. "A lullaby for *brothers.*"

FOUR

"Hold still," said Annie Burton. "At least let me fix your collar before you go."

The sun had not yet reached its peak on a breezy Saturday morning, and the smell of salt water wafted in from the edge of the cliffs. Cole stood back and waited while his mother fiddled with Tinn's shirt, brushing a bit of lint from his shoulder before she was satisfied.

"Nobody in the horde is going to mind a few wrinkles," Tinn said, but he allowed his mother to fuss over him just a little longer. He knew the ritual wasn't about the shirt.

It was time for Tinn's weekly trip to his *other* family—to the horde at Hollowcliff. The exchange was never easy. It had taken a long time for Annie to get comfortable leaving her son in the care of goblins, even just for an afternoon, but she knew these visits were important to Tinn. Chief Nudd had given her every assurance the boy would be kept safe, and the goblin Kull dutifully prepared lessons every week that seemed to be helping Tinn grow more comfortable and confident in himself, not to mention more capable with his changeling magic. There were things that Annie could not teach her son, and things she would never understand about the man he was growing into—but Tinn would always be her little boy.

"What do you think you'll study today?" said Cole.

"I never know going in," said Tinn. "Kull likes to mix it up. One time he had a whole group of friends come in to help teach me a traditional Goblish folk dance. It was neat to watch—but there was a lot more biting and headbutting than I had been prepared for, to be honest."

"Just promise me you'll be safe." Annie brushed Tinn's shaggy hair out of his face.

Behind her, Kull and his usual goblin escorts were just emerging from the hidden path on the cliff's edge.

"I'll be fine, Mom." Tinn gave her a big hug.

"Don't have too much fun without me," added Cole.

"Say hi to Fable and Evie for me," Tinn said. "Meet you all by the cabin after lessons?"

Cole nodded. The quiet clearing had become their usual rendezvous point.

Soon, Tinn was marching off down the path with Kull, while Annie and Cole stood alone on the bluff. Annie put her arm around Cole's shoulder, and the two plodded back through the woods.

"You boys are growing up so fast," she said as they walked. "You're going to be taller than I am in no time."

Cole smiled at her. "Was dad tall?"

She nodded. "Tall and strong, with big broad shoulders, just like you're shaping up to be."

They walked a few paces in silence.

"Do you ever think about him anymore?"

Annie took a slow breath before answering. "I do. Not like I used to, though. I used to think about him all the time—the way he would press his forehead against mine when he hugged me, how he smelled after he shaved, how he loved to make hot chocolate after a hard day."

Cole put an arm around his mother's waist, and she looked down at him as if coming back to herself from far away.

"Over time," she continued, "I guess I began to think more about where he might be and what he might be doing, and then eventually about all the places that he *wasn't*—all the events that he was missing. I think about what he would have said to you boys on your first day of school and what he would've done for your birthday when you turned ten years old. I think a lot about the man he would've been for you. For all of us." She squeezed Cole's shoulder a little tighter. "It's been so long. Sometimes I wonder if I'm really thinking about him at all anymore, or if I'm only thinking about some version of him that I've created in my mind. And then I look at you and I see your eyes crinkle in just the same way his used to and he comes back to me all over again."

Cole leaned into his mother and they held each other close while the forest slid slowly past them.

Gradually the sound of voices began filtering through the trees ahead. "That's Fable," said Cole. "It sounds like Evie's already with her."

"You'll be careful today?" Annie said, tucking a strand of hair behind Cole's ear. "No wandering into brownie nests or going swimming in cursed pools?"

"I promise," said Cole.

"And you'll come right home with Tinn when he's all done? I'll be at work until nearly sunset. I do not want you boys out here when it gets dark."

"We were going to walk Evie back to her place first, but we'll come right home after." Cole gave his mother a hug and hopped off the path to go join Fable and Evie in the Wild Wood.

Annie bit her lip. One of her boys was hanging off a cliffside with a horde of goblins, and the other was frolicking through an enchanted forest with a witch's child. These were not the parenting choices she had imagined herself making thirteen years ago when she had sung the twins to sleep in their crib.

"Hi, Cole," said Evie. "What's that?"

Cole glanced down at his hand. "Oh. It's nothing."

The stone, roughly the size of a half-dollar, fit comfortably in his palm. On its face was carved a thick central column with branches forking out and leading up to a domed top, like a simple tree. Cole rubbed the etching with his thumb, tracing the rough pattern for the thousandth time. He couldn't remember deciding to take it out of his pocket—but there it was again.

"It's not nothing," said Fable. "That's the extra-special rock that the spirit of the spring gave him."

"Whoa," said Evie. "What's it do?"

"It doesn't do anything," said Cole.

"It's got something to do with his missing dad," Fable said. "Probably. Maybe. It's super mysterious. Kallra never gives *me* special rocks. Everybody else gets the cool presents."

"What does the symbol on top mean?" Evie asked.

"I don't know," said Cole.

"Nobody knows," said Fable. "That's what makes it so mysterious."

"The spriggans know," Cole mumbled. "One of them got really angry when he saw it."

"What's it got to do with your dad?" Evie pressed.

"I don't know that, either." Cole frowned. "I saw him in the reflection right before Kallra gave it to me." He ran his thumb over it one more time, feeling the etching beneath his touch. "He's out there somewhere."

"Maybe," said Fable.

"Kallra shows the future, not the past. And I saw him. That means he's alive. He *will be* alive. Whatever. He's out there."

Fable turned to Evie. "Where did that spriggan say he had come from?" Fable asked Evie.

"What?" said Cole. "You told me you hadn't seen any spriggans for weeks."

"I hadn't," said Fable. "And then I did."

"He said he came straight from a burrow in the Oddmire," said Evie.

"Oh. Right. Sorry, Cole," said Fable. "Even if we could get through the Oddmire without it turning our brains all wonky, we still don't know where to find it."

Cole's eyes lit up. "But we do know someone who might."

"He's always around here somewhere," said Fable. They had been walking up and down the bank of the Oddmire for the better part of an hour. They had seen a pair of pixies, a hob, and a hedgehog that Fable introduced as Squidge—but no Candlebeard.

Cole slumped down on a mossy boulder. "Maybe we need to try from the eastern bank?"

Before Fable could answer, the rock Cole was sitting on shuddered. He hopped off just as the boulder unfolded itself with a grinding crunch into two arms, two legs, and a scowling, rocky face.

"Troll!" said Evie.

"Human sit on Knurch!" the troll growled. It stalked forward with heavy, thudding steps. "Knurch sit on *human!*"

"Hey! What do you think you're doing?" Fable yelled.

The troll glanced up. "Little Queen," he said. "Knurch wasn't going to *kill* humans."

Fable crossed her arms.

The troll looked as sheepish as a craggy chunk of rock is capable of looking. "Knurch was maybe going to kill *one* human," he mumbled. "Only little bit."

"Seriously?" said Fable. "There's a truce on! Who's the troll king?"

"Kurrg the Ruthless," answered the troll.

"And what did Kurrg the Ruthless say about killing humans right now?"

"To not do that." Knurch shuffled a foot, effectively carving a small ditch in the soft soil.

"That's right. And Kurrg the Ruthless is friends with my mama. If you think *he* would've been mad at you for breaking the rules, you don't want to know what my mama would've done to you. Now, maybe you can make it up to me by telling me if you've seen my friend around. He's a hinkypunk."

"Knurch help Little Queen," the troll grunted. Then he turned, cupped his hands to his mouth with a clink, and bellowed: "HINKYPUNK, COME FIND SMALL, SQUISHY FRIENDS!"

All three children slapped their hands over their ears, and a flock of birds took flight from the trees behind them. "He come," said the troll. The troll nodded and hunkered back down, folding itself back into a knobby boulder.

Sure enough, a minute later a light bobbed into view through the distant fog. The creature hopping from hidden step to hidden step along the surface of the swampy waters was more beard than body, and from within the bristles of that beard, the light of a stubby candle flickered.

44

Hinkypunks were not known for being reliable guides—but this one had a debt to repay, and Cole knew it.

Candlebeard was barely ashore when the kids rushed to explain the situation, one speaking over the other, until they had told him everything, concluding with their need to find the spriggans' burrow. The hinkypunk scratched his long, scraggly beard and looked out over the misty, murky waters of the Oddmire. He looked apprehensively from Fable to Cole to Evie.

"You know where it is, don't you, Candlebeard?" said Fable.

The furry fellow nodded unenthusiastically.

"Please?" said Cole. "Will you show us the way?"

Candlebeard looked pained.

"My dad is out there somewhere," said Cole. "The spriggans might be the only ones who have the answers we need to find him."

Candlebeard chewed on his whiskers. At length, he gave an almost imperceptible nod. Without further discussion, he hopped straight out into the mire, landing on an invisible stepping stone just below the surface of the muck. He bounded forward, and again his foot found purchase on an invisible support.

"I don't know about this," Evie said, eyeing the wide gaps between the hinkypunk's hidden steps and the burbling, sucking muck that awaited any traveler who missed their mark. "Didn't you tell me that the last time you followed a hinkypunk path, Tinn almost died and you all got stranded in the middle of the mire?"

"Yup," said Fable. "But that was before I could do *this*."

With a squelch, a series of roots rose out of the muck, forming a knobby platform wide enough for all three of them to stand on. Fable stepped out onto it, and Cole joined her. More cautiously, Evie followed. The landing was not as elegant as the woven bridge that her mother could manufacture, but it was sturdy, and it held their weight above the muck.

Candlebeard glanced back for just a moment to be sure they were following, then set off again, skipping from one hidden perch to the next.

Fable tensed her fingers, and the roots of her platform extended farther out over the mire, forming a path to follow the hinkypunk. As the children stepped forward, the rear end of the magical bridge sank back into the mud. Evie felt the cords beneath her begin to sag, and she hurried to stay close on Fable's heels. And so they proceeded, step by step, into the mists of the Oddmire.

"Oof. Does this fog make anybody else's brains feel all . . . bendy?" asked Evie after they had left the shoreline behind them.

"That's normal," said Fable. "Well—normal for the Oddmire."

Cole could feel his head starting to spin, too. He had forgotten just how disorienting the mists of the mire could be. Fable kept the living platform inching forward, and whenever they began to lag behind, Candlebeard mercifully paused to allow them to catch up.

Time passed strangely within the mire, but it could not have been more than a few minutes before they reached the muddy shore of an island. The land mass, no more than twenty feet wide, was covered in ferns and prickly bushes. Cole glanced back. The mists rolled and curled in his vision. He could no longer see the forest they had left, nor could he see any proper land in any direction. Out here, there was nothing but the mire and the mist—and the island.

Candlebeard stopped short of the muddy beach. His eyes looked pained, and he shook his head, as if advising the children against going ashore.

"We'll be okay," said Fable. "Don't worry."

Evie was the last to step off the roots and onto solid—if rather spongy—ground. She nearly lost her footing as she did, and Candlebeard held out a hand to steady her.

"Thank you," she said, accepting it. Then she blinked and swayed. "I'm sorry. What was your name again?"

Candlebeard's eyes flicked meaningfully down toward his chin. From within his beard, the candle flame danced.

Evie shook her head. "I'm usually good about names. Sorry. My head feels all funny."

Candlebeard nodded and gestured out at the mire, where the mists swirled and the trees seemed to bend and sway in the distance.

"He's saying it's the mmmist that mmmucks with your head," said Fable. The words felt all rubbery in her mouth and the Ms got stuck on the way out.

"I don't like it," said Evie.

Candlebeard glanced left and right, as if the mossy trees creeping out of the mire might be watching him, then leaned over to the edge of the island and pulled a few yellow weeds. They looked a little like dandelions with smaller dandelions growing out of their middles. Candlebeard plucked off a few blooms and handed one to each of the children.

"Oh," Evie said. "Um. That's very nice. Thank you."

Candlebeard shook his head. He held up another flower and popped it into his mouth, chewed for several seconds, then swallowed it.

Evie blinked.

Candlebeard pointed to the flower in her hand, then at her mouth.

"You want me to . . ."

Candlebeard nodded.

Evie lifted the flower to her lips and took a hesitant nibble. Its petals tasted faintly sweet at first, but as she chewed, the flavor turned powerfully bitter.

Candlebeard gave her a satisfied smile.

"I'm not sure what this is supposed to—" Evie stopped. "Oh." She looked around. Had the world stopped tilting? The trees that faded off into the mire suddenly seemed to stand a little straighter. "This flower clears your head, doesn't it?" she said.

Cole and Fable exchanged a glance and then munched on their own flowers. In a moment, all three children were blinking and looking around as if awakening from a dream.

"That's brilliant," said Evie. "Thank you, Candlebeard. I'm going to write a special note about this in my journal later."

"Let's get this over with," Cole said. "Thanks again, Candlebeard. We'll be right back."

As the kids pushed their way through the foliage, a small clearing came into view. In the dead center of the island was a circle of stones. It looked a bit like a well, except that the stones were not stacked neatly like a human-built structure—they simply jutted out of the earth in a natural, uneven ring. Within the rocky halo was . . . nothing. The ground simply gave way to a deep tunnel that bored straight down into the earth. It sank far deeper than the surface of the mire all around them, and Cole had to wonder what kept the swampy waters from seeping in.

"I guess this is the Oddmire Burrow." Cole stepped forward first. He approached the circle slowly.

"What is it?" whispered Fable. "What did we find?"

Before Cole could answer, a rasping voice called out from in front of him.

"Death."

FIVE

"OTCH! YER NA EVEN TRYIN' TODAY!" KULL threw up his arms. "Where's yer head at, lad?"

Tinn sagged. The uneven spray of feathers that had been blossoming from his arms drooped. "I'm sorry, Kull. I'll try harder. I think I just need to take a break."

They had been practicing transformations—usually Tinn's favorite subject. Having gotten comfortable with imitating most humanoid forms, Tinn had been the one to suggest he should *stretch his wings*, so to speak, by adding some animal characteristics to his repertoire. Early attempts had been clumsy, but at least he had managed a few of the right shapes. Today, he looked like a lanky thirteen-year-old who had rolled around in a chicken coop.

He slumped into a chair at the table, willing his arms back to their usual texture.

Kull eyed him. "Hm. All right. Out with it."

"With what?"

"Ya couldn'a focus on yer Goblish composition earlier, either. You kept mixing up yer dashes and yer hashes. And ya didn'a even touch yer brotblath during lunch—an' I put extra flowers and moss in it for ya today."

"You also put a whole squirrel in it."

"Yer a growin' boy. Growin' boys need good protein iffin they don't want ta be growin' numpties who make all sortsa mistakes because their heads is miles away."

Tinn sighed and slumped down on the table with his head in his now-featherless arms.

"All right, lad. Out with it. What's on yer nogg?"

Tinn took a deep breath. "Cole, I guess."

"Yer brother? What's he done now?"

"Nothing. It's just . . ." Tinn's stomach felt twisted.

"Have ya talked ta him about yer Turas yet?" Kull asked.

The Turas Bàis was a goblin coming-of-age ritual that Kull had brought up a few lessons ago. It was a dangerous journey every young goblin had to take before they could become an adult, and they had to take it alone.

Tinn shook his head. "I've tried to bring that up a couple of times. There's not an easy way to tell your family that you're thinking about going on a huge trip without them for months. Especially when that trip is literally a *death journey*."

"Otch. I should never have told ya the translation. A Turas is na about dyin'—it's about putting ta rest the part o' you that's already passed, lettin' go o' the corpse o' the *old* you so the *new* you can stand tall on his own two feet. Technically, Goll the blacksmith came back with just the one foot ta stand on, but not every Turas is as exciting as Goll's. Besides, he made himself a shiny new one in no time." He sat down across from Tinn. "Every goblin takes a Turas, lad. When the time is right an' the goblin is ready . . ."

"I'll find the right time," said Tinn. "But that's not what's bothering me." He slouched back against the worn wood of the chair. "We've been looking for our dad together—our human dad—Cole's dad."

"Mm." Kull nodded. "No luck, then?"

Tinn shook his head. "No. We haven't found a single real clue. Nobody has, not for years. We might never. Cole thinks he found one, but it's just a sort of rock. The whole thing feels weird anyway."

Kull raised an eyebrow in question.

"It feels weird looking for somebody who ran away

because of what you are. I'm finally getting to enjoy being . . . me."

"Ah." Kull winced and nodded again. "So why do ya keep looking?"

"It's really important to Cole. It's all he talks about. He's convinced that our dad's out there somewhere. And if he is—well—then he owes Cole some answers. He owes both of us some answers."

"And what if they're na the answers ya want to hear?"

Tinn shook his head. "Cole deserves to know, one way or another." He glanced down, and his voice became a mumble. "*I* deserve to know."

Kull's brow furrowed. He had blotchy green skin, flopping leathery ears, and teeth like broken glass—but every once in a while when he looked at Tinn like that, the goblin's face reminded Tinn of his mother. It was the eyes, all full of concern. Not that Tinn would ever tell his mother that. Kull's eyes lowered as he spoke: "Just be careful, lad. Sometimes when ya dig up the past, ya find more bones than ya buried."

Tinn just stared down at the parchment littering the table, the wrinkly paper covered in hash marks and blotted ink from his Goblish writing lesson.

At length, Kull slapped the table and stood. "Enough o' this for today. Come on, lad. Nearly time for yer appointment with Chief Nudd. You know he likes ta hear about yer progress."

Tinn slid out of the chair and hurried to keep up with Kull as the goblin padded out the front of the cave and onto the gangplank that hung along the face of Hollowcliff.

When they reached the chief's cave, however, they found it guarded by a sentry in what Tinn was beginning to recognize as female goblin armor. (The difference was that female goblin fashion tended toward having slightly thicker leather and more rodent skulls.)

"Hullo there, Gnubb." Kull nodded to the goblin, who tipped her head in greeting. "Got us an appointment with the chief."

"Chief's oot," Gnubb said. "Hasn'a been back since last night."

"He's out?" said Tinn. "But he never misses our meetings."

Gnubb shrugged. "High Chief has a lot o' responsibilities. He canna put havin' a blether with a wee child over whatever urgent matter come up."

"Hrm. Thass fine," Kull said. He turned back to Tinn with a shrug. "Gives us time enough for a few more lessons! Oh, and I got just the one ta take yer mind off yer troubles."

"What's our next lesson?" Tinn asked as Kull led him back down a series of rickety hanging bridges.

"Secret sites." Kull smiled. "Nothin' ta get yer mind off

of one mystery like buryin' it in another one. Besides, time you learned a bit o' goblin geography. After that, iffin we've still got time, we'll try ta squeeze in a good sneakin' lesson."

"I'm already good at sneaking," said Tinn.

"Yer good for a human. Rubbish for a goblin. I'll teach ya ta proper sneak."

The salty air whistled over rocks and through the caverns all around them as they made their way into a narrow opening farther down the cliff.

"How many caves are there in Hollowcliff?" Tinn asked as they wound through an unfamiliar tunnel.

Kull shrugged. "We're always carvin' new ones, expandin' old, sometimes poppin' our heads up in another goblin's bedroom on accident. Mistakes happen. Onward and upward. Or downward. Or a bit sideways. Ah. Here we are."

After a few craggy bends, the tunnel opened into a wide room with a low ceiling. On the walls hung elegant tapestries, framed canvases, and humble yellowed papers pinned with simple tacks. On all of them were maps. There were colorful maps and simple sketches, finely detailed maps, rough world maps, and maps of places Tinn suspected were not of this world at all. In the center was a round table decorated with yet another map, this one depicting a forest and a familiar coastline.

"That's the Wild Wood," said Tinn.

"Aye." Kull nodded. He pulled a blank sheet of parchment and a charcoal pencil from a drawer. "Copy her down, then, lad," he said. "Best ya can. Mind yer lines."

Tinn laid the paper on the table as he began to sketch a miniature version of the Wild Wood. "We must be . . . right here, on the cliffside," he said as he scribbled. "And here's the Oddmire running through the forest, and that's got to be Endsborough over there." There were no labels on the table map—not in Goblish or any other language— but symbols dotted the terrain.

"That's right," said Kull. "What else d'ya see?"

"Lakes, pixie rings. That looks like a satyr over there, and that one below it is definitely a wolf—I'm guessing that's the Warg to the south. Does the little picture over there mean troll territory?"

"Good! And the bit above it is yer wee Fable's new common ground. Be sure ta add that in." Toward the upper half of the map was a small clearing with one big tree in the center. The symbols of several factions were huddled together in the space. "Times change, but we keep the cartography up ta date." Kull smiled proudly.

"Maps at home just make the forest look like a bunch of trees right up until the ocean. This makes the whole Wild Wood look so . . . full."

Kull's eyes glinted. "Aye. It is that. This lesson isn'a

about the things ya know, though—it's about lookin' for secrets. Find yourself a secret."

Tinn scanned the map again. His eyes paused in the upper right corner. "Is that a castle peeking out of the bushes up there?"

Kull clapped. "Good! Aye. It's only ruins now—but it was grand in its time. Beautiful buttresses, fine brickwork, quality death traps. That's a castle you'll na find on any non-goblin maps. What else d'ya see?"

Tinn looked again. "There's a lot of islands I don't recognize."

"Go on."

"What's that one circled in red?"

"Oooh." Kull grinned broadly and rubbed his hands together. "Now *that* is a secret site! The Isle o' Bones. One o' the forbidden isles. Shrouded in mystery."

"It's made of bones?"

"Aye. Well. Some bones. Mostly dirt and rocks and broken garbage—but also bones! Lots of bones! At least twenty, maybe thirty percent more bones than the average island."

"Is it a graveyard?"

"Like none you've ever seen. There are bones of goblins and humans and all manner o' fair folk, all mixed up and discarded like broken toys. No one knows how they got there. The island itself wasn'a always there. The merfolk an' the selkies say it just rose from the ocean floor, inch by inch. It reached the surface thirty or forty years ago, and it grows larger every year. No faction claims it. None visit it."

"That's creepy."

"Proper creepy. We goblins used ta sail out to it from time ta time, scavenging the surface lookin' for useful relics. Then one day a couple years back, they found the remains of a goblin wearing a special ring—the signet of Chief Gwynn. Nudd's father."

"It was his dad?"

"It was his father's advisor, Wenn. She'd been like an auntie to Nudd. She vanished years ago, when Nudd was still a young goblin. The old chief sent out search parties and tore the Wild Wood apart looking for her. I was young then, too, but I can still remember it."

"How did she wind up buried on a mysterious island?"

Kull shrugged. "Therein lies the mystery. Bones is just bones—but it's a little scarier not knowin' how the people ya care about *became* bones. Nudd declared the island cursed and quarantined after that. We're na allowed to go pokin' about no more."

"Whoa," said Tinn. "Goblin geography is way more interesting than human geography."

Kull looked pleased with himself. "Wanna see the relic room?"

The dim chamber that he led Tinn to next was lined with broken tools and bits of clothing and armor. The only light came from shafts cut diagonally up to the surface, piercing the gloom every five or six feet with columns of dusty light. They walked between rows and rows of dead people's property. There were no bones in the collection, but still the air felt heavy with the weight of lives lost. A dented shield, taller and heavier than Tinn, rested on one countertop, and beside it sat a pair of boots so small Tinn could have barely fit his pinky fingers into them.

Tinn walked farther into the room. He recognized some items as common goblin tools, and others he could not identify at all. There were relics that looked human-made, too. A shovel with a broken handle, a pair of eyeglass frames, a dented red lunch box.

Tinn stopped.

The lunch box was dirty and rusted, but it looked exactly like the one Winston Bell had tucked in his locker at the Echo Point Mine. Tinn stepped closer. The box had something inscribed on the lid, too, just under the layers of dust. Tinn could feel his heart beating faster. He reached out a hand and wiped away the dirt. An icy jolt sizzled down his spine as he read the letters: *J.B.*

Joseph Burton.

SIX

"DEATH," CAME THE RASPING VOICE AGAIN, AND finally Cole's searching eyes found a source. A spriggan no taller than Cole's outstretched hand stood perched on the rocky opening to the tunnel. It was perfectly camouflaged, its armored skin the same slate gray as the stones around it and a cape of moss draped over its back. In one hand it held a barbed spear.

A quiver of motion all around the mouth of the entry-way told Cole that there were probably many more of the diminutive guardians watching him. He had only spotted this one because it wanted him to.

"I need to talk to you," said Cole.

"I suspect"—the spriggan's voice was cold and eerily calm—"that what you *need* is to continue breathing and to keep your blood inside your veins."

Cole swallowed.

"What *you* need," Fable said, stepping forward to Cole's side, "is to stop threatening my friends."

The spriggan eyed her for several seconds before responding. "We do not wish your companion's death," it said. "But we will deliver it. You stand on a threshold. To cross into this sacred territory is forbidden. Even for you, witch. Your mother understands this. *She* would know better. Now leave . . . or die."

As if on cue, clouds rolled in overhead, darkening the scene. The mists of the Oddmire seemed to be swirling around them more quickly, too, as if the mire itself were growing anxious.

"I think," Evie whispered behind them, "we should do what they say."

"We don't want to enter your sacred grounds," Cole called out. "I have something here that I don't understand, but I think that you might. It's important." As he fumbled in his pocket for the stone, a muffled chittering arose around the cavern, and half a dozen pairs of steely eyes materialized as tiny heads rose to watch him closely.

"Here," Cole said, producing the artifact. He held it up for the nearest spriggan to see. "Can you tell me anything about this symbol? Please, I need to know."

The little guardian's eyes widened, and it turned its stony face from the symbol to Cole and back to the symbol. The whole ring around the cave erupted into motion. At least twenty spriggans rose from the terrain, weapons drawn and muscles tense.

"He dares," hissed a voice toward the back of the group.

"Kill them," grunted another.

The spriggan at the front held up a hand, and the chatter quieted. "You have brought an unholy thing to a sacred place," it rasped. "Explain yourself."

Cole felt Fable's hand on his shoulder. He took a deep breath. "All I know is that it has something to do with my father."

"Then your father is dead. Or worse. And so will you be unless you leave this place at once."

"No," chirped a shrill voice from the swarm. "We cannot let them live. They will summon the darkling."

A chorus of chirps and chitters rippled through the group.

A tall spriggan with a vest of woven twigs hissed and banged its spear against the rock. "Cowards. It is not right for spriggans to fear the darkness."

"It *is* right to fear the Ancient Ones," the shrill voice spat.

"Superstitions and stories," growled a grizzled white spriggan with a cloak of cobwebs. "The Ancient Ones are long dead."

"They have only slumbered. And they are rising."

Voices overlapped as the swarm erupted into a cacophony of arguing.

The first spriggan took a step closer to Cole and looked him up and down with narrowed eyes. "Take that wicked sigil away from here," it rasped. "Destroy it. Bury it. It can bring you no good."

A few of the angrier-looking spriggans were whispering together and moving closer to the children.

"I think we should go," Evie whispered, tugging at his arm, "before they change their minds."

"But what *is* it?" Cole tried one last time.

"It is a promise," said the spriggan. "Pray that it is never kept."

Fable took a step away from the cave. "Come on, Cole." She and Evie pressed back the foliage as they edged their way toward Candlebeard's path.

Cole tucked the stone back into his pocket and nodded. "Fine. I'm going."

Dozens of sets of glistening, wary eyes followed his

every motion. Jagged spear tips remained trained on him as he took one step and then another away from the entry. He paused. He turned back.

"The thing is—"

But before Cole could finish his thought, a heavy blow caught him from behind, and he fell forward, tumbling uncontrollably toward the mouth of the forbidden cavern.

SEVEN

Tinn HURRIED DOWN THE GOBLIN PATH through the Wild Wood. Thoughts echoed around in his head, each one humming like a piano string—except they came together less like structured chords and more like an instrument tumbling down a stairwell.

What did it all mean? How had their father's lunch box ended up on a mysterious Island of Bones? Had Joseph Burton gone there in search of something? Had he been taken there against his will? Did this mean that their father was among the dead?

Tinn was halfway back to Endsborough before he

remembered that Cole would not be there. He had been planning to spend the afternoon with Fable in the forest while Tinn was busy with his lessons.

Tinn adjusted course and made his way instead toward the clearing near the old cabin in the woods. The clearing was empty when he arrived, but the bushes to the eastern side rustled as he approached.

"Cole?" he called. "Fable?"

A craggy rock troll stumped through the bracken. "Human is looking for Little Queen and her squishy friends. Won't finds them here. Won't finds them anywhere, most like."

Tinn scowled. "What do you mean by that?" he said.

The troll shrugged. "Hinkypunks play tricks." He shrugged. "Oddmire play tricks, too." His granite eyes narrowed. "Spriggans don't play at all."

Tinn stared for several seconds. "They wouldn't."

The troll bobbed his head.

"Show me where they went," said Tinn. "Please?"

The troll raised an eyebrow. "Why would Knurch help human?"

"Because," said Tinn. "Because . . . if you do, I'll tell the Queen of the Deep Dark you helped look out for her daughter's safety. She's sure to be grateful."

The troll looked unconvinced.

"And if you don't—I'll tell the Queen of the Deep Dark that you *didn't* help look out for her daughter."

The troll seemed to turn a slightly paler shade of gray. "This way."

A few minutes later, Tinn was standing on the banks of the Oddmire. Sure enough, he could see several sets of footprints in the mud, all leading straight into the swampy waters.

He certainly wasn't going to step right in hoping to find a hidden hinkypunk path all by himself. The last time he had tried following Candlebeard through the mire he had nearly drowned.

Tinn paced up and down the bank for several minutes, listening to the distant buzz of insects and the whistle of the wind through the trees all around him. A blue jay fluttered onto a tree branch across from him and tilted its head as it watched him.

Wait. That was it.

Tinn straightened. He took a deep breath. He held out his arms and closed his eyes as he concentrated. A warm tingle of magic rippled up and down his arms as he focused on the shape. Bird wings. Big, like an eagle's.

He felt a pinch of pressure as the bones within his arms

shifted. He held his breath. The breeze picked up, and he could feel the wind beneath his feathers.

He opened his eyes and flexed his new appendages. They were so much longer than his regular arms, but they looked just as Tinn had pictured. Yes! His best wings yet! They responded intuitively, bending and stretching, but they felt so heavy.

Kull had mentioned something about the weight when they had first started practicing—what was it? Right. Birds have hollow bones to keep them light enough to fly. Tinn concentrated again, and inside him, his entire skeleton tickled. It was an unsettling sensation, but when it was done, Tinn could feel himself sway in the air currents.

This could work.

Cautiously, he climbed up on a nearby log and stretched out his wings. "Here goes nothing."

With a little hop, he took to the air and coasted in a wobbly arc down to the ground.

"Okay." He allowed himself a smile. "Pretty good!"

The blue jay cocked its head and looked unimpressed before flapping away.

"Right. *Up.* I can do *up.*"

Tinn took a little running start and flapped his arms. At first he didn't seem to be gaining any altitude at all, and then he caught too much air and nearly spun himself backward. With a few more tries, he was able to get himself airborne. He coasted along the edge of the clearing until his feet were brushing the grass, then flapped again, just a few times. It worked. He felt the wind under him like a gentle pillow. This time his body lifted with almost no effort at all.

"I *can* do this," he said aloud, beaming. "I really can!" He took a deep breath, stretched out his wings, and pushed off into the sky.

The swirling mists of the Oddmire rolled around Tinn as he flew. The trees that grew out of the muck were sickly things, few and far between, easy to navigate around. This was working.

The muscles in his arms felt hot and the mists made his eyes water, but he pressed on. Just a little farther. If he still didn't see anyone, he would turn back.

A flicker of light caught his eye. Tinn veered toward it, and soon a dark shape began to form in the fog ahead. It was an island—and on its shore was a little bald man with a candle right in the center of his enormous beard. Tinn opened his mouth to call out in his excitement, but then hesitated as the rest of the island came into view. Right in the center of the land was a wide cave, and at its mouth . . .

"Cole!" Tinn's words were swallowed by the wind. Cole's attention was on the mouth of the cave, and he made no indication that he had heard. Tinn's muscles were beginning to burn with the effort of keeping aloft, and his vision was starting to spin. It was the mist. He needed to get out of this mist.

He angled his wings downward, feeling heavier by the second. He was coming in too fast. As he rocketed toward his brother, he tilted his arms to try to counter the momentum—arms. Oh, crud. He shot a startled look at his arms, covered in long eagle feathers, but decidedly human and not birdlike.

Between Tinn and the rapidly approaching ground stood Cole. Arms flailing, helpless to change course, Tinn bowled into his brother from behind at full speed. He felt the breath knocked out of his body in a wheezy whoosh, and the two of them tumbled toward the mouth of the cavern.

EIGHT

THE SPRIGGAN'S NAME WAS CLOVERMOSS. IT DID not suit her. Her older brother had been clover-bound, covered with a vibrant coat of green all year round. Her older sister, too, had been blessed with foliage—a lively tunic of natural lichen that came in around her third decade. Clovermoss, however, had never shown so much as a sprout.

Not that there was anything wrong with stoneskin. Some of her closest friends had stoneskin—but they also had fitting names like Jadeshine and Avalanche. Clovermoss had never loved her name, but from a young age she had determined to make something of it. She excelled in her training and had been highly decorated for her service during the gnomish riots in the year of the Appletree. Clovermoss had spent her life ensuring that when any spriggan uttered her name, it would be not with scorn, but with pride and awe.

And so it was Clovermoss who had been assigned the role of chief guardian the day the children approached the sacred Oddmire Entry. There had been only three trespassers to set foot on the secret island in more than a century. Two of them had been injured birds who had collided in midair, confused by the mists. The third had been a young and foolish hinkypunk, one whose family cluster had collected him promptly, bowing low in apology as they scurried away across the mire. Clovermoss was keenly aware that if these humans crossed the threshold now, it would be a historic failing.

It complicated matters further that the "Little Queen" was with them. Bringing the fury of the girl's mother—the Witch of the Wood—down on the nest was almost equally unthinkable. The truce had been tested enough in recent months. So it was with tremendous relief that Clovermoss watched as the children finally retreated.

"Fine," said the boy. "I'm going." He turned and took one step, and then another. But then he paused and glanced back.

Clovermoss tightened her grip on her spear. All around her she could sense her comrades tensing for action.

"The thing is—" the boy began.

And then, abruptly, a fourth figure exploded out of the sky above them in a tornado of flapping arms, fluttering feathers, and kicking feet.

The half boy, half bird barreled into the first boy from behind, sending both of them tumbling, skidding, and rolling straight into the open mouth of the forbidden cavern. For half a second time slowed as the two clutched at the slick rocks, trying to prevent the inevitable fall.

Clovermoss stared, openmouthed, as a matching pair of panicked faces disappeared over the lip of the cavern and plunged down the steep drop, straight into the sacred spriggan underground.

Clovermoss could feel the weight of her reputation plummeting alongside the boys. Little Queen or not, there could be only one response to the transgression.

"Well?" she rasped, when she found her voice at last. "Kill them!"

The boys fell. Rocks and roots and damp earth raced past them on every side. The passage bent beneath them, and in a blur they were suddenly sliding and bouncing, crashing against the walls of a dark tunnel—and then the walls were the floor, up was down, down was sideways, and the whole world was spinning. And then the boys came to a stop.

Tinn could hear Cole panting beside him.

"Are . . . you . . . okay?" he managed.

"Tinn?" Cole groaned and righted himself. "Oh no. This is bad."

Tinn blinked. It was not fully dark in the tunnel beneath the mire. All around them the earth glowed with the faint light of a thousand tiny, glistening gems, sparkling pale blue dots nestled within the soil. It was like looking up at the open sky on a clear winter night. In the hazy glow, Tinn could see paths and corridors, much too small for anyone their size to navigate. This cavern was not made for human beings. The two of them might be the first humans to ever see this far into a spriggan burrow.

"This is very, very bad," said Cole.

Tinn followed his brother's gaze upward. A circle of gray defined the opening high above them. Shapes moved in the space between, and the circle became clouded. Tinn's eyes gradually made sense of what he was seeing. Scores of spriggans were pouring down into the tunnel after them. They came in a chittering, descending swarm, hopping from wall to wall as they neared. Tinn winced as a sharp pain shot through his arm.

"Ow!" He glanced down and saw a barb as long as his

index finger sticking out of the skin. Another stinging bolt suddenly shot into his leg. "Hey! Ouch!"

He glanced up at his brother in time to see a ribbon of bright red appear on Cole's cheek as a jagged spear cast him a glancing blow. "Ugh!" Cole grimaced and held a hand over his face. Almost at once two more ivory javelins lodged themselves in his arm.

"Stop!" Tinn yelled. "Please! Help!"

Tinn's head was spinning. The blood running down his arm was hot and the pain was everywhere. In another moment the whole swarm would be upon them. Another sharp, hot pain in his shoulder. Was this the end? How long would it take?

And then the cold swept past.

It whipped from the depths of the cave behind the boys and up into the open air high above. In a wave, the twinkling lights of the cave blinked out. A dark blanket of shadows rose around the brothers like an inky tide. The shadows swept along the walls of the tunnel, rising out of the depths of the cavern as they surged upward.

Tinn heard his brother gasp, and then he heard the frightened shrieks of the spriggans above them. He strained to see what was happening. Dozens of the tiny guardians were now scrambling back up the sides of the tunnel as the darkness threatened to overtake them.

A woody spriggan with armor like tree bark lost its grip, and a tendril of darkness swallowed it up at once, pulling the struggling shape down and into one of the narrow side tunnels. Another, its skin like chipped granite, lost its footing and yelped once as it fell backward into the sea of liquid blackness.

The icy chill enveloped Tinn, and he shuddered. He had felt this cold only once before, in the heart of the Deep Dark. No. It couldn't be. *The Thing.*

In another second, the inky wave swelled, and Tinn's vision went black. His whole body felt numb and weight-less. He reached for Cole, but he could not feel anything. He hung helplessly in space, unable to speak, unable to even breathe, his mind reeling.

The Thing had returned to finish what it had started last year. Tinn had been a fool to set it free—but at the end it had seemed such a pitiful creature, shivering with fear in the palm of his hand. This time there could be no rescue, no forest folk coming to his aid, no mother finding him in his moment of need—not here, not now. The Thing had them.

And then the darkness ebbed to gray.

Tinn felt his heart pounding hard against his chest, and he gasped for a breath. Beneath him, he could feel soil and grass. He was not dead.

His fingers tingling with cold, he pushed himself up to sitting and clawed at the thin veil of shadows that clung to his face. The stuff stuck to his fingers like spiderwebs, but bit by bit it fell away. Tinn shook his head, panting.

Cole was there beside him, tearing sheets of darkness from his own head and shoulders. The scraps melted into the earth where they fell. Tinn looked around. They were not in the tunnel anymore. The wave of darkness had deposited them safely back at the mouth of the cave.

"What . . . just . . . happened?" Cole huffed.

Tinn watched as the last of the shadows slunk back into the tunnel. There was no sign of the spriggans. There had been droves of the little guardians—but now the opening to the tunnel was barren. A leaden lump rested in Tinn's stomach, and he thought he might be sick.

Sensation gradually crept back into his skin, and with it came the burning of dozens of bleeding cuts and fresh bruises. Dully, he realized a familiar voice had been calling out from behind him.

"Come ON!" Evie yelled.

And then she was holding Tinn by the arm and Fable was there, too, guiding Cole away from the tunnel, and the four of them were pushing their way through the bushes. A very bald head with a big, bushy beard was waiting for them as they emerged once more on the shore of the little island.

"Candlebeard," breathed Cole. "You waited."

A few minutes later, all five of them were free of the murky mire and standing once more on solid ground in the relative safety of the Wild Wood.

NINE

THE ROOFTOPS OF ENDSBOROUGH PEEKING
through the trees were a welcome sight as the children
finally crossed over the trickling stream that defined the
western edge of the Wild Wood. The sun was beginning
to sag in the sky, and the noisy chirping of crickets sur-
rounded them.

"Mama wants me to be back by sundown," said Fable.
"Are you sure you'll be okay from here?"

"We'll be fine," said Cole, trying hard not to look like
he felt—as if he had been run over by a building.

They bade Fable goodbye, and the remaining three of
them slogged onward up the winding path toward town.

"It's pretty neat that you got the bird thing to work," said Evie, finally breaking the silence.

"It might need a little practice," said Tinn.

"Still," she said. "You should be proud. I'd be proud."

Her hand slipped into his as they walked, and Tinn's aches and pains faded to the back of his mind. Even in the cool dusk air, he could feel his ears get hot.

A twinge of guilt crept into the back of his skull. He hadn't told Evie he was thinking about his goblin Turas yet, either. How do you even start a conversation like that? The times he was with Evie were times when he *least* wanted to go away.

He gave her hand a squeeze, and she leaned in.

"Can you become any kinda animal?" she asked.

"Hm? Oh. I think so," said Tinn. "With enough practice."

"Could you make yourself tiny? Like a ladybug or something?"

"It doesn't work that way," answered Tinn. "It's all still the same *me*, just squished around into new shapes."

"What do you think they meant—*It's a promise?*" said Cole.

"Huh?" said Evie.

"The spriggan said, *It's a promise.*" He was a few paces ahead of them, holding the stone up to catch the setting sunlight along the lines of the etching as he walked. "A promise of *what?*"

Evie shrugged. "I don't know. One of the spriggans said there was an *Ancient One* and that it was *rising*. I'm not sure what that means, but they seemed pretty spooked about it." She gave Tinn's hand one more squeeze and then let it go as they took the left fork in the path. Her uncle's farm was just around the bend.

"Whatever it is, it doesn't explain anything about our dad," Cole sighed. He finally tucked the stone back into his pocket. "Maybe it doesn't have anything to do with him after all. I just . . ." He kicked a dirt clod on the side of the path. "I'm so stupid. For all that trouble, we're not any closer than we've ever been. I just risked all of our lives over a rock—and for all I know, Dad just hitched a ride years ago and skipped town. Maybe he's in Glanville or New Fiddleham right now, selling sausages out of a cart."

Tinn stopped walking. Cole and Evie turned to look at him. Tinn took a deep breath. "I don't think he went to New Fiddleham to sell sausages . . ."

Cole and Evie listened in silence as Tinn explained about the goblins' Island of Bones, the mysterious artifacts that manifested in its soil, and the old red lunch box with their father's initials carved into the top.

When he was done, Cole was quiet for a long time, his expression clouded.

"Secret island?" said Evie. "Well. I know where we're headed next."

"You did hear the part where I told you that it's cursed, right?" said Tinn.

"How convenient," Evie said, "that I happen to know somebody who knows more about curses and mysteries than anyone else in the whole wide world." She turned her eyes to her uncle's farmhouse. "Wanna come in and say hi?"

The clock on Old Jim's mantel ticked loudly as he looked the boys up and down. The man's thick, bushy eyebrows cast heavy shadows over his eyes. A fire crackled away in the hearth, keeping the house almost uncomfortably warm, and the whole place smelled strongly of sage and burnt coffee grounds. Little bundles of dried herbs tied up with twine were strung by the door, and a silver cross hung by a single nail. The walls were decked with charms and talismans, and a set of shiny crystals sat on the windowsill, catching the evening light. One might have mistaken this collection for ornaments, if not for the sturdy metal blades, traps, and cages that shared the shelves with them.

"See. That right there"—he gestured vaguely at the myriad cuts, scrapes, and greenish bruises covering the twins' faces and arms—"is why I'm not keen on you running around all day in that infernal forest, Evelyn."

"We fell down," said Cole.

"There was a hole," said Tinn.

"Mm-hmm." Old Jim regarded them both through narrowed eyes. "I'm sure there was. The two of you seem to find no end of holes you need help digging yourselves out of."

"Evie's fine," said Tinn.

"I can see that she is. If she wasn't, you boys would be wishing you had stayed in your hole." Old Jim cast them one more meaningful look, and then he cracked his neck and stood up. "Well. I suppose I'll go fetch the iodine and see if I don't have a roll of bandages around here somewhere to patch you fools up."

"Uncle Jim," Evie said as he rummaged in a cabinet at the back of his kitchen, "we were wondering—do you know anything about . . . islands?"

"I know you want nothing to do with the waters off the coast around these parts. The forest is dangerous enough, but at least the monsters in there stand on solid ground and breathe air like you and me. The sea is a whole different mess." He banged a brown medicine bottle on the counter and opened another cupboard.

"What's off the coast?" asked Tinn.

Old Jim grunted. "There's serpents so big they can crush a ship in half. And wild water horses who drag men to the bottom of the ocean just for fun. Finfolk are even more devious. They act all nice and feed you a special plant that helps you breathe underwater—but the longer you stay down there, the more you forget. Eventually you can't even think for yourself anymore, and then they own you. Nasty monsters, all of them. Here we are." He produced a roll of cotton bandages from the back of a shelf. "What on earth you fool kids want to know about islands for, anyway?"

"For . . . my book?" said Evie with a weak smile.

"My foot," said Old Jim. "Fine. Don't tell me."

"For my dad," said Cole.

Old Jim's eyes narrowed again. "If you're gonna tell tales, kid, that's one thing—but don't you dare go using your old man as part of your mischief. He was a good man."

"He's alive," said Cole. "And there's an island somewhere off the coast where he might be. The goblins stumbled onto proof. You can believe me or not, but it's true. It's covered with bones, and it's probably cursed, and I don't even know if we'll be able to find it—but it's all we have."

"Then all you have is nothing."

Cole clenched his fists. "You *knew* him." He raised his chin and looked Old Jim in the eyes. "You said yourself he was a good man. We never got the chance to learn that for ourselves. He's *our* dad and he was taken from us."

Old Jim let his gaze fall to the floor. "Lotta folks in town think otherwise," he said.

"*You* don't," said Cole.

Old Jim pursed his lips.

"He *didn't* run away," said Cole.

"I know he didn't, kid." Old Jim took a deep breath. The room fell quiet, save for the ticking and the crackle of the fire. Old Jim rubbed the back of his neck as he regarded the children each in turn. "I might know a guy with a rowboat," he said at last.

Evie straightened. "Really?"

"But there's no way in tarnation I'm sending you kids off on your own to get drowned or eaten or Lord knows what."

Cole glanced at Tinn. Tinn swallowed. "Are you going to tell our mom about this?"

"Do I look mad?" Old Jim shook his head. "I like my chances with the finfolk and the kelpies better'n with your mother if she knew I was offering to take her boys out to some cursed island. You want to go off half-cocked, hunting for trouble—you're stuck hunting it with me this time. That means for once in your fool lives you boys are gonna listen to me and mind what I say. Understood?"

Two identical heads nodded in unison. Evie could barely contain her grin.

"One week. Meet me right back here at dawn next Saturday, if I haven't come to my senses."

TEN

THE SUN HAD NOT YET CLIMBED OVER THE EAST-
ern hillside when the twins rounded the bend and reached
the Warner orchard the following week. Old Jim was
already outside hitching a pair of bay workhorses to a wide
cart on which a faded tarpaulin stretched over the shape of
a trim little boat.

"I'll sit next to Tinn," said Evie. Tinn felt his face go all
warm. He could transform to look like anyone in town, but
he still couldn't stop his cheeks from going all red whenever Evie was around.

"Yer gonna ride up front with me," Old Jim said. "And
the boys are gonna slip under the tarp in back and keep

hidden until we're clear of town. Unless you want to wave to your mother as we pass the general store?"

"Wait—we're taking the main road out?" said Tinn. "But that's the opposite direction from the coast."

"What, did you think we were going to just plow straight through the whole dang forest and then jump off a fifty-foot cliff?"

Straight through the forest was precisely how Tinn had gotten to the coast nearly every week for the past year. The goblins had ships secretly moored at the bottom of the steep cliffs, with hidden stairways that led down to them— but it had not occurred to Tinn that there might be a less clandestine route to reach the ocean.

Soon the boys were listening to Endsborough rattle by from under the boat. They could hear a murmur of voices and smell bacon frying as they rolled past the Lucky Pig. For just a moment, Tinn considered changing his mind, calling the whole thing off, running to tell his mother everything—but the moment passed and Endsborough faded into the distance. A few minutes later, Old Jim let them know they could come out if they wanted to.

They both climbed up into the front, and the rest of the trip went by in a blur. Evie sketched in her journal along the way, and Old Jim examined the map that Tinn had copied down, making note of where they would be setting off and how far it was to the mysterious island.

Old Jim unfolded a map of his own, an official one with color ink and a fancy seal. Tinn couldn't help but feel a little self-conscious about his hand-drawn sketch, but Old Jim seemed satisfied that the two lined up fairly well, point for point.

"If your drawing is right," he said, "then this mystery island of yours shouldn't be too far off the cape. Can't imagine why a hundred sailors coming in and out of the bay every month wouldn't have spotted it. We should be able to make it there and back without too much trouble."

"And if we don't find anything?" said Tinn.

"Then we don't find anything," said Old Jim.

The packed dirt became bumpy bricks as they rolled into the port at Abbot's Bay, which looked a bit like some giant had taken a big C-shaped bite out of the coastline. Along the top of that C was the cape—a long stretch of land that reached far out into the waves like a knobby finger pointing the way to their destination. Old Jim paid to have his horses fed and tended to while they were out, and soon the four of them were sitting in the squat rowboat, pushing off from the dock and into the gray salt water.

Cole watched the water rippling beneath them as Old Jim rowed. The waves lapping against the sides of the vessel felt like low, rolling hills. At first it seemed as though they were making no progress at all, but before he knew it, the dock had shrunk to a speck in the distance and the cape was growing larger and larger.

"We're getting closer," said Evie. "Anybody see anything yet?"

They turned their eyes toward the choppy waters beyond the end of the cape. Where the strip of land ended, a series of jagged rocks began. The water splashed and sprayed against them like gnashing teeth.

"Nothing you could call an island," said Tinn. "Just rocks."

"Don't get too close," Old Jim cautioned. "Give 'em a wide berth. One big swell would be enough to smash us against those suckers and tear the bottom clean off this skiff."

They peered across the water, trying to make out any land beyond the rocks. The sunlight bounced off the waves in blinding flickers and flashes, illuminating nothing but the occasional sharp rock piercing the surface.

"There's nothing out here," said Old Jim. The water clapped against the side of the boat in a slow, steady tattoo. "Sorry, kids. Like I said, a hundred sailors coast past this spot every month. If there was an island, it would be common knowledge. Oof! Mind the rocks, Cole. Getting a little close, there, kid."

"Sorry," Cole pushed and pulled against the oars to redirect the boat. "I'll take us farther out."

"Wait," said Tinn. "Do you hear that?"

Silence hung over the boat for several seconds as they all strained their ears. They heard the lapping of the waves against wood, the distant call of gulls . . . and an unfamiliar, muffled clink of metal on metal.

"What is that?" said Evie.

"It's coming from that way," said Tinn, squinting against the glare coming off the ocean.

"Nothing that way but nasty rocks waiting to split open a hull," said Old Jim. "Maybe an old chain got washed up on one of them? Stay clear. Not even an experienced sailor would go through there on purpose."

Tinn's eyes widened. "Which is why none of them ever do."

Old Jim raised a bushy eyebrow. "That's what I just said."

"Could you get us in, just past the first few rocks at least?" said Tinn. Jim raised an eyebrow. "The goblins discovered the Island of Bones, and nobody else had a claim to it. They would've put their charms on it."

"Charms on what? There's nothing there, kid."

"If goblins want you to stay away, they take something you already want to stay away from and just sort of nudge the feeling farther. I can feel it, nudging us away. That means there's something there to nudge us away from. Please."

Old Jim's scowl deepened. "This right here is why I hate all this dang magical hoopity-doopity. I don't like having my head messed with." He gripped the oars tightly. "Hold on—this might get bumpy."

Carefully, he rowed the skiff between the jagged rocks.

"My head feels funny," said Cole as they slipped farther into the hazardous waters.

"Mine, too," said Evie. "Kinda tingly."

Directly ahead, the air was growing thick, as if clouds were forming in midair. The sea before them began to blur. "We're almost through it," Tinn said.

And then the veil fell away. The island did not appear, exactly. It had always been there, but their eyes finally stopped refusing to see it. Tinn had grown accustomed to this magic—he had even been allowed to watch Chief Nudd casting a similar spell when the horde repaired the northern watchtower on the cliffside.

"Whoa," said Evie.

"Well I'll be—" said Old Jim.

The island was about an acre wide, as broad across as the sloping cow pasture that the boys sometimes cut through on their way into town. Unlike the pasture, there were no tufts of hay or wildflowers blossoming at the edges. While it was not made of bones, as its name implied, the Island of Bones was undeniably a dead place.

Instead of trees or grass, there were great heaping mounds of debris, rising and falling in hills and valleys, and the air was thick with dust. Crushed gravel and fine brown dirt covered the surface, and sticking out of it were cracked helmets and scraps of cloth—here a dented canteen, there a rusted old wheel attached to the frame of a broken cart. .

Old Jim brought the boat aground and, reverently, the four of them stepped onto the desolate shore.

"Was there a shipwreck, do you think?" whispered Evie.

Tinn shook his head. "Doesn't look like a shipwreck."

Cole hiked ahead toward the highest mound, right in the center of the island. He stepped past a torn glove sticking out of the dust, a belt buckle with a brass boar's head, and a silk vest so big he could've used it as a blanket. Out of curiosity, he nudged the fabric with one foot. Ivory-white ribs beneath told him that whoever had worn that vest had not taken it off. He tore his eyes away.

At the top of the mound he found the head of a pickax and a tool that might once have been a narrow spade, only the metal had been bent backward. A corner of what appeared to be a steel box stuck out of the gravel. Cole nudged it, but it was buried deep in the rocky soil. It didn't budge.

94

The wind picked up and swept across the surface of the eerie island, and the metallic clinking resumed. By Old Jim's knees, the top of a bent iron ladder protruded diagonally from the ground, and from it hung the chain of a long-dead pocket watch. He reached down and picked it up. Its face was smashed glass, and one of the hands was missing entirely.

Old Jim grunted. "Tigani pocket watch. They used to sell 'em cheap at Cobb's Outpost."

"I don't think they ever sold *these* at Cobb's Outpost," said Evie. She held up a pair of goggles by an intricately woven leather strap. Even if they had been working, they would have been much too small for a human head. A series of hinges controlled half a dozen lenses that swung into place in the front, but these were now bent beyond repair. Most of the lenses were cracked or missing, but, even covered in dust, the metal shone like it was glowing.

"Those are gnomish," said Tinn. "I've seen a pair like them at Hollowcliff. They have a set for analyzing gems and stuff."

"None of this stuff belongs," said Evie. "Where do you think it came from?"

Before anyone could hazard a guess, the island began to tremble beneath them. A cascade of rocks tumbled down from the mounds, and with them a few smaller relics rolled and bounced to the surface.

"Watch out!" yelled Old Jim. He grabbed hold of the half-buried ladder to steady himself. Tinn stumbled, landing hard on one knee. Evie fell next, and soon Cole was sliding down the middle mound on his back.

In another moment, the tremor died down and the island fell silent once more. The dust was gradually settling.

"That was a big one," said Evie.

Cole pushed himself up, then stood for a moment, gazing at something small in the palm of his hand. With a start, he glanced back up at the top of the mound. The corner of the thick metal box he had kicked was now almost fully unearthed. It was no box—it was a sturdy black mine cart with a broken axle. "I know where it's all coming from," he said.

"What do you mean?" said Tinn.

"Below," he said. "It's coming from below."

"From where?" said Tinn. "The bottom of the sea?"

Cole held out his hand and allowed Tinn to pluck from it a tiny, glowing, blue stone. "Where have you seen gems like that before?"

"The spriggan tunnel. It was lined with them."

"And a lot of these tools look like they belonged to miners. Human and otherwise. What if the spriggan tunnels and the human tunnels are actually connected?"

"No way," Evie breathed.

96

"The goblins have whole networks of tunnels, too," said Tinn. "They don't even use some of them. Kull says they're just bricked off because they dug too deep."

The ground shook a second time, sending a fresh cascade of detritus rolling down the mounds. It tapered off with a shudder, and the four of them coughed in the resulting cloud of dust.

"Time to get out of here," said Old Jim. "You kids got your peek. I don't know if it's a curse or just a quake, but I'm not waiting around for this island to fall apart on top of us. Go on, back in the boat."

Another shudder, and a grisly skull emerged from a nearby rock heap and rolled to a stop at Cole's feet.

"I said back in the boat," barked Old Jim. "Move it."

He waited until all three children were in before giving the vessel a shove and hopping in to take the oars. In the aftermath of the earthquakes, the whole bay was rolling with frothy waves that slapped against the jagged rocks. The boat tipped and lurched, fighting against Jim as he rowed—but he managed to navigate back into open waters, and soon the currents calmed and the boat steadied. When Cole dared to glance back, the island had once again slipped behind a curtain of invisibility.

ELEVEN

Bᴦ ᴛʜᴇ ᴛɪᴍᴇ ᴛʜᴇ ᴄᴀʀᴛ ʀᴀᴛᴛʟᴇᴅ ʙᴀᴄᴋ ɪɴᴛᴏ Endsborough, the shadows of the trees lining the road had already melted together into a prevailing dim, and hints of orange were beginning to highlight the wispy clouds above them.

During the slow, rolling ride, Evie's head began to dip, and finally she rested it on Tinn's shoulder. Tinn felt his face go warm all the way out to his ears, and he couldn't help smiling for the whole last leg of the journey.

"Here you go," said Old Jim, drawing the horses to a stop. "Landslides and killer waves are one thing, but I ain't facing that mother of yours. You boys can brave her on your own."

Annie Burton was sitting at the kitchen table when the boys slipped through the door. She did not get up. Her expression was tight and her lips were pursed.

"Hi, Mom," said Tinn.

Annie did not reply.

"Sorry we're late," said Cole. "We were just—"

"Don't," she cut him off. "Not one more lie." She took a deep breath. "Do you have any idea how worried I've been? I spoke to Raina, so I know you weren't with Fable this afternoon. She tracked down Kull for me, so I know you weren't at the horde, either. You weren't anywhere in town. You weren't out by your climbing tree or the old bridge, and you obviously haven't been home. So before you give me one more clever story, consider—for once—just telling me the truth."

Tinn glanced at Cole. Cole nodded to Tinn.

"We went looking for answers about Dad," said Cole.

Annie's eyes closed. "Your father is gone," she said. "It's time for all of us to accept that."

"He's underground," Cole said.

"You don't know that," sighed Annie, pained. "You *can't* know that for sure."

"But I do," Cole said. "He's underground. And he's alive. I *am* sure of it."

Annie was silent.

Cole straightened and took a deep breath before continuing. "And we're going after him."

Annie turned her head slowly from Cole to Tinn. "Anything to add?"

Tinn bit his lip and lowered his eyes. "It's true," he said. "And other people have gone missing, too. Fable says her mom's been dealing with disappearances from loads of different forest factions. And Chief Nudd hasn't reported back to Hollowcliff in days. That's not like him. Whatever took dad is taking people again, but there's a real chance that we can find them." He looked at his brother. "That we can find *him*."

Cole nodded. "So there it is. That's the truth. We're going to find Dad."

He waited for his mother to raise her voice—waited to be scolded, to be grounded, to be told a hundred reasons that going after their father was going to get them killed.

Silence hung over the house for several seconds.

"Yes," said Annie Burton. "We are."

Tinn finally looked up from the carpet. "*We?*"

Annie Burton crossed her arms. "Together. No more secrets. No more sneaking around."

"You're not going to tell us not to?" said Cole.

"Would it do any good?"

Cole and Tinn exchanged another glance.

"That's what I thought." Annie leaned back in her chair. "Okay," she said. "Tell me what we know."

And so the boys told their mother everything. The sky outside their windows had dimmed from a pale gold to deep purple by the time the Burtons finished talking.

"All right," said Annie Burton at last. "Get some rest. Tomorrow we make plans to get your father back."

Soon after, Cole and Tinn were tucked snugly into their beds, each of them clad in clean pajamas, their foreheads recently kissed and their hair freshly ruffled. They lay quietly in the moonlight for several minutes before Tinn spoke.

"It doesn't feel real," he said. "It's not just you and me messing around anymore. Looking for Dad used to feel like when we were kids and we went searching for pirate treasure in the cow fields. Now it feels like . . . like something else."

Cole nodded. "Are you afraid?" he said. "It's okay if you're afraid."

Tinn stared at the big tree outside their window for several seconds as it swayed gently under the stars. "Do you really think we'll find him?"

"I hope so," said Cole. "Do you?"

Tinn glanced across the room. His brother's eyes sparkled in the moonlight. He hadn't seen Cole so hopeful in months. "Of course I do." Tinn's throat tightened.

And what if they did? He stared at the ceiling as crickets chirped outside. What would Tinn ever say to a man who gave up everything just to be rid of him?

TWELVE

"Let's go over what we know," said Annie Burton. The boys sat on one side of the breakfast table, nibbling strips of bacon, while Annie sat on the other, a cup of dark tea cooling beside her. Between them were a small stack of blank paper and a stubby pencil. "We know there's something lurking under the ground, stealing people and then pushing up the leftovers into a big pile of bones and garbage off the coast."

"We also know they pushed up Dad's lunch box," said Cole, "but they didn't push up *Dad*. And I saw him alive in Kallra's future-vision, so we also know he's still out there. Most likely underground, too."

"Right," said Annie. "So whatever snatched your father and all the rest of them must have some sort of secret, underground lair deep beneath the forest, and even deeper than the ocean."

"A lair that even the scariest creatures in the Wild Wood are afraid to get close to," added Tinn. He slipped a piece of bacon to Chuffy, the chubby black house cat, who purred contentedly and rubbed against his leg.

"Which is a good sign that the scariest creatures in the Wild Wood are a lot smarter than we are," said Annie. "But if we're doing this, then how do *we* get close to it?"

"Hm," said Cole. "We could try to tunnel down through the island to whatever is pushing the stuff up?"

"Okay," said Annie. She made a note on her paper. "Lots of digging. High chance of drowning, but that is one route. Any other ideas?"

"The spriggan caves?" said Tinn.

"Right." She wrote it down.

"Spriggans *kill* trespassers, though," Cole said. "They already want to kill us. And we'd have to get past them in order to get to . . . well, whatever else will probably want to kill us down there."

Tinn nodded solemnly.

"Any other options?" said Annie.

"The goblins?" Cole suggested. "If we explore those

tunnels on Hollowcliff, we might find one of the ones they sealed off. The ones where they dug too deep."

Tinn smiled.

"See? I listen," said Cole.

"That does sound a little better." Annie added it to the list. "We know the goblins, at least."

"But humans aren't allowed in horde territory," Tinn said. "Kull might be okay with it, but a lot of the rest of them would get mad if I tried bringing you in with me, and with Chief Nudd gone, they're all on edge already. Plus, supposing I could get you into the horde, even goblins aren't supposed to enter the sealed tunnels. They're off-limits."

Annie's brow furrowed. "So—not ideal."

"The mines," said Cole. "It's got to be the mines."

It was quiet for a moment as each of them waited for one of the others to raise a counterpoint against it.

"That boarded-up shaft looked like it went down a really long way," said Tinn.

Cole nodded. "It's probably how he got down there."

Annie pursed her lips. She used to be a miner's wife. She knew only too well about coal dust and toxic fumes and cave-ins—all very good reasons to stay out of condemned shafts, especially if you enjoyed things like breathing and having a heartbeat. She closed her eyes. Not *used to be*.

She *was* a miner's wife. He was still down there. He was still alive.

"The mines it is," she said.

It was midday when the Burtons reconvened at the kitchen table.

"Mr. Zervos was very understanding, all things considered," Annie said. "I suppose it doesn't hurt that I spent half a month's wages stocking up on supplies."

"What did you tell him you were leaving for?" asked Cole.

"Did you tell him you were sick?" suggested Tinn.

"Family vacation?" said Cole.

"I told him the truth."

"Wait. Really?" said Cole. "The real truth?"

"Yes. I told him my boys were getting increasingly reckless without my supervision, and that I needed to spend some time with them as a parent before they went off without me and got themselves killed."

"I can see how he might have believed that," said Tinn.

"Fable came by while you were out," said Cole. "I told her we wouldn't be able to play today because we're getting ready for the big search. She thinks you're super awesome for going with us."

"That's because I *am* super awesome," said Annie. "Fable is an excellent judge of character—but maybe don't go telling any more people about this. Okay, let's check our supplies before it gets too late for me to run into town for anything else." Annie plucked the stubby pencil from behind her ear. "Let's see. Two pickaxes. Two coils of rope . . ."

Cole picked up some rope. "Oof. This is heavy. How long is it—a hundred feet?" He slid his head into the coil so that it hung over his shoulder and across his chest like a bulky sash. "How do I look?"

"Like you're ready for anything," said Tinn. "As long as the thing you need to be ready for is having rope."

"Two safety lanterns," Annie continued. "Half a dozen candles. Waterproof matchboxes." She pointed to each of the items in turn as she ticked them off on her list.

"Ooh. Trail mix!" said Tinn. "Think fast!" He tossed a bag to Cole.

"Is it the kind with chocolate chips?" said Cole, catching it and peeking inside.

"Put it down." Annie marked the trail mix off her list. "Three bags of travel provisions. One tin with half a dozen sandwiches, one large package of beef jerky."

"Is that enough sandwiches?" said Tinn. "Maybe we should make more sandwiches."

"It's plenty of sandwiches. We're not planning on staying underground forever."

"Can I have a piece of jerky before we go?" said Cole.

"No," said Annie. "Those are for the trip."

A sharp knock pulled all of their eyes to the door.

Annie put down the list and crossed to the front of the house.

Tinn and Cole peeked around her as she opened the door.

Annie straightened.

"Hi. It's me," said Old Jim. He shuffled his feet awkwardly on the front step, Evie at his side.

"Mr. Warner." Annie crossed her arms. "I see you *do* remember how to talk to your fellow adults after all."

Old Jim winced. "I take it the boys let you know my part in yesterday's business?"

"You mean the part where you took my children with neither my knowledge nor my permission and put them in harm's way a hundred miles from where I could do anything to help them?"

"Forty miles," mumbled Old Jim. "Maybe forty-five. Tops."

Annie raised an eyebrow.

"Say the thing you *practiced*." Evie nudged her great uncle's leg.

Old Jim cleared his throat. "I owe you an apology," he grunted. "Should've told you first. That's on me."

"You shouldn't have gone at all," said Annie.

Jim rubbed the back of his neck. "I know. I only . . . But, no. You're right. It was downright irresponsible to take them kids marching into something dangerous that I didn't fully understand myself."

Annie's steely gaze faltered for a moment. "That's right," she said. "Completely irresponsible."

"What's that for?" said Evie, pointing at the rope wrapped around Cole's chest.

"This? It's for climbing," Cole said. "And probably for other rope-related stuff. You never know."

Jim looked at the rope. He looked at Annie. His eyes narrowed. "Foolhardy, even," he said, more slowly.

Annie swallowed. "Indeed." Over her shoulder, the table of supplies was just visible.

For several long seconds, the adults locked eyes.

"What's happening?" Evie whispered, looking from one of them to the other.

"Whatever it is, we're in," said Old Jim.

"What? No—" Annie began to protest, but Old Jim stepped past her into the house before she could argue. Evie followed in his wake.

"So, what's the plan?" said Old Jim.

"Really! Jim—" Annie tried, but he was already crossing into the kitchen to survey the supplies.

"We're going to Echo Point," said Cole, following him through the doorway. "We're going to try to find a way down through the old tunnels."

"Cole!" Annie glared at him. Cole shrugged.

"Mm." Old Jim's head bobbed in approval. "Good call. Folks talk about hearing things in those tunnels all the time. They've got to connect to *something* down there. We bringing anything to protect ourselves?"

"Jim, seriously—" Annie said.

"Mom bought us those couple of pickaxes," said Tinn. "And some trail mix."

"Is it the kind with the chocolate chips?" asked Evie.

Annie threw up her arms in exasperation. "Of course it's the kind with the chocolate chips!" she yelled, quite a bit louder than she had intended to.

The room quieted for a moment as Annie leaned heavily on the countertop with both hands and took several steadying breaths. "Look. I appreciate the offer, but Joseph is *my* family," she said. "I can't ask you to come with us."

Old Jim put a gentle hand on her shoulder. "No one asked for your help before you jumped into the bucket brigade when the stationery store caught fire, did they? They didn't need to. Your boys didn't need to be asked for help

110

when they pulled my sorry butt out of the line of fire during that battle a few months back, either. You and yours
might stir up more'n your share of trouble, but you never
hesitate to stick your necks out for me and mine. So I'm
not waiting to be asked. You're fixing to finally find Joseph?
We're in. End of discussion. Ain't that right, Evelyn?"

Evie grinned.

Annie's shoulders sagged. "Fine," she sighed. "You're
in." The twins grinned.

Before anyone could add anything, another sharp
knock rattled the door.

"Who now?" Annie made her way to the front door
again.

Fable was there, beaming merrily. "Hi, Annie Burton!"
On the stoop behind her stood Raina, the indomitable
Queen of the Deep Dark.

"Fable? Raina?" said Annie. "Is everything all right?"

"My daughter informs me that you intend to embark
on a perilous journey into fathomless subterranean depths
beneath my Wild Wood," Raina said. Her voice was as cool
as the autumn breeze.

"Well." Annie hesitated. "I wouldn't phrase it quite like
that."

"We are coming with you."

"Excuse me?"

"I do not feel that I need to repeat myself," said the queen. She stepped past Annie into the now increasingly crowded house. "We are ready to depart when you are."

Fable smiled broadly as she followed her mother inside. Annie blinked.

"I think," Tinn said softly from beside her, "we're gonna need more sandwiches."

THIRTEEN

LAMPLIGHT PLAYED ACROSS THE ROCKS, CAST-ing arches of pale, flickering gold along the walls and ceiling. Heavy wooden beams had been erected every fifteen feet or so to reinforce the roof, but they slanted at odd angles, giving the passage a dizzying, twisted atmosphere. The tunnel was cool and smelled like dirt and damp. The party moved forward in relative silence, but every footstep they took echoed and fractured into a dozen muffled copies of itself, filling the tunnel with a dull, wordless susurrus as they progressed.

"It's through here," said Cole.

They had waited until nearly sundown—not that daylight would make any difference where they were going. The final whistle had blown almost an hour ago, and the last employees of the Echo Point Mining Company had finally left.

Annie eyed the broken boards and faded warning signs as her sons led the way into an abandoned mine shaft. "Really?" she said. "You thought coming through here unsupervised was a good idea?"

"It's not much farther," said Cole. "Watch your head."

"I don't like it," mumbled Old Jim. "This whole place is creepy."

"It's not so bad," Evie tried. "I mean. It's just a hole in the ground, if you think about it."

"Hrmph," Jim grunted. "Get to my age and you start thinking a lot more about winding up in a hole in the ground. I've never been too keen to get into one any sooner than I need to."

"Watch your step," said Tinn, up ahead of them. "It slopes down."

Annie glanced over at Raina, who had not spoken since they crossed the property line into Echo Point. "Are you all right? You've been quiet."

"I'm fine," said Raina.

"That's her *not-actually-fine* voice," whispered Fable.

114

Raina gave her a barbed glance. "We are moving farther away from my forest," she admitted. "I can barely feel my trees anymore."

"Ah," said Annie. "Does it help if you think of it as just a deeper part of the forest?" She tried to keep her voice comforting in the gloom. "I mean—Evie is right, this is only a hole in the ground. If you dug a hole and buried a seed in it, it would grow into a new part of the forest, wouldn't it? It's all connected."

"If you dug a hole and buried a seed at *this* depth, it would *die*," said the queen flatly.

Annie did not have a motivational answer to that.

"This is it!" called Tinn.

Everybody circled around as the boys pulled the last few broken boards away from the deep chasm that had almost swallowed them a week before. When they were done, just one sturdy crossbeam remained intact, a four-by-four, fixed by thick iron spikes to the rocky floor of the tunnel. The light of several lanterns could not pierce the gloom all the way to the bottom of the shaft.

"You nearly fell down *that?*" said Annie. "What were you *thinking?*"

"It was a mistake," said Tinn.

"Everybody makes mistakes," said Cole.

"You don't make very many if you make 'em that big,"

said Old Jim, tossing a pebble down the shaft. It fell a very long time before it ticked against the rocks below.

"At least we've got rope this time," said Cole.

"Mm," Old Jim grunted. "The fall ain't the only thing that can kill you. Evelyn and I brought protection, in case it turns out we're not alone once we get down there."

"No guns," said Annie. "We talked about this."

Raina narrowed her eyes at Jim and put a hand reflexively to her chest. Jim had not been the one to pull the trigger, but it was his rifle that had nearly ended her life in the battle at the forest's edge. The scar still had not fully healed.

"I know. No guns." Jim held up his hands defensively. "Wouldn't want to cause a cave-in, anyway. I'm not an idiot. Show 'em what we packed, kiddo."

Evie stepped into the light. She and her great uncle had swung by his place before the trip, and they were now wearing matching vests covered in pouches—the sort hunters and fishermen in town liked to use to store spare ammunition or tackle. Evie's was much too big for her, but she didn't seem to mind.

"I brought all sorts of useful things," said Evie. She unbuttoned a few pouches as she got going. "We both packed a bulb of garlic and a small onion, because everybody knows those are good at warding off evil things, and I picked us some of those plants that Candlebeard showed me the other day, the ones that help clear your mind. They're called bitterwort, apparently. This pouch here has a little salt in it, and this one has wild rose petals. Let's see. I also brought an iron railroad spike and a silver knife. It's only a butter knife, but it's real silver, and that's the important bit."

"That's my girl," said Old Jim proudly.

"Who's going down first?" said Tinn. He was gazing into the darkness at the bottom of the shaft.

"Me," said Annie. She shifted the pack on her back. "It should be me."

"Okay." Jim nodded. "Let's get you strapped up."

Soon, one of the ropes was looped around the beam and passed to Annie. She drew the rope between her legs and over her shoulder as Jim instructed. She would rappel down the shaft, using her body to gradually release the cord until she reached the bottom. The spare rope, it was decided, would be tied around her waist just in case the first failed and she needed to be caught.

Six sets of hands carefully helped lower Annie Burton into the darkness.

Cole hardly breathed until he heard his mother's voice call: "I'm at the bottom! I made it! I'm okay!"

"What's it like down there?" Fable yelled. "Any monsters?"

"There's a lot of dark," Annie called. "I could do with a little less of that, if you don't mind."

They felt the emergency line go slack, and they pulled it up quickly and tied the rope to the lantern's handle. They lowered it down until Annie could grab hold of it.

"I see the wood and broken glass from the lantern that the boys dropped," she called up. "And there's a tunnel down here. It's definitely big enough for someone to walk through it."

"Just wait for us to join you," Old Jim called down. He turned back to the group. "Who's next?"

"I'll go," said Cole.

The rope bit into his leg, but it was easier to control his descent than Cole had feared. His feet soon touched solid ground, and his mother was immediately there to steady him. He looked around.

Beside them was a tunnel at least as tall as he was. It did not have any of the man-made supports or tool marks of the paths above them. The walls were smooth and a bit lumpy, more like a natural lava flow. It went on for a long way, and the light of the lantern did little to pierce the gloom of the natural passage. His eyes scanned the ground. He wasn't sure what he was expecting to find. A footprint? A torn piece of his father's clothing? In the dancing light of the lamp he saw nothing but rocks and dust.

One by one the rest of the party made their way to the bottom of the shaft, and soon only Old Jim remained up above. He lowered the second lantern to Evie before finally joining the rest of them.

"Welp," he said, dusting his hands off on his trousers, "nobody dead or broken yet. Good job so far. Hey now, wait for us!" This last he yelled after Tinn and Evie, who were already twenty feet down the next tunnel.

"Come on, then," said Tinn.

"It looks like it opens up a little farther ahead," Evie called.

The walls all around them looked as if they had been carved by some enormous worm tunneling its way through solid rock. Raina was shaking her head, her eyes narrowed and her brow creased.

"You okay?" said Annie.

"We shouldn't be here," said the queen. "I can feel it. Wards. Protective charms. There's old magic in these tunnels. And it is not my magic."

"Something doesn't want us going forward," Annie said. "Unfortunately, that sounds like a pretty good sign we're going the right way."

Raina nodded, but she did not look happy.

"The path forks up ahead." Tinn's voice echoed back to them. "There's three more tunnels to pick from!"

By the time Annie and Raina joined the rest of them in the next cavern, Cole had already drawn a wide chalk C on the wall of the tunnel they had come through. "So we can find our way back if we get turned around," he said.

Annie couldn't help but smile. It was a clever habit that had helped her catch up to the boys when they had first gone off into the Wild Wood without her.

"So, which one do we try first?" said Fable.

"We could split up and check all three," suggested Tinn. "Then meet back here in a few minutes?"

"No!" said Annie and Raina at once.

"We are not splitting up," said Annie.

"Splitting up is a bad idea," agreed Old Jim.

"Let's just try the one in the middle first," said Annie. "All together, okay?"

They trod carefully down the central corridor, hand in hand so nobody could get lost. That, at least, was the plan—and it was a good plan, right up until the earth suddenly shook, the ground crumbled beneath their feet, and all seven of them plummeted in a frantic free fall into a yawning abyss.

FOURTEEN

Tɪɴɴ sᴄʀᴇᴀᴍᴇᴅ ᴜɴᴛɪʟ ᴛʜᴇ ᴀɪʀ ʜᴀᴅ ʟᴇꜰᴛ ʜɪs lungs, and still he was falling.

The pit that had opened beneath them was wider than the spriggan tunnels—even wider than the first shaft they had descended to get into this mess.

"Tinn!" his mother's voice cried from somewhere nearby. "Take my hand!" He reached out blindly, trying to find her, but his wrist slapped against a sharp rock as he fell, and he pulled it back to his chest. His breaths were coming in gasps. He could scarcely tell up from down as he plummeted into the dark, and his mother's voice was soon swallowed by the roar of wind and echoing voices. He could hear the frantic cries of his friends and family bouncing off of the walls all around him until—worse—he couldn't hear anything at all.

His ankle smacked against another rock in the gloom, sending him into a wild spin as pain blossomed through his leg. Flashes of light flickered in his peripheral vision, but he had no time to focus on anything before his back slammed into something broad and solid and the wind was knocked out of him.

Still he fell.

He couldn't see anything, and even if he could, it was all moving too quickly. The stony surface whipping past him sloped more and more as he fell past it—until eventually he was not falling past it at all, but rolling along it, and soon the wall felt less like a wall and more like a steep hill, and then like an uneven floor. Tinn tucked his chin to his chest to keep his head from slapping against the rocky ground as he slid, at long last, to a stop.

He lay, dazed—unable to move, unable to breathe—for what felt like an eternity.

How far had he fallen? A hundred feet? A thousand? Somewhere in the distance he could still hear the clatter of rocks, their echoes piercing the heavy silence in an uneven rhythm. Eventually he managed to gulp a lungful of air, and then another. He heaved shallow gasps in the pitch-black underground.

He was, for the moment, alive. Any more than that he would have to confirm later. A light blossomed in the darkness somewhere nearby. He tried to turn his head toward its source, but his muscles refused to respond.

"Hello?" came a frightened voice. "Is there anybody there?" It was Evie, her words trembling.

Tinn willed himself to sit up, to wave, to call out to her. His body stubbornly ignored every instruction.

"Tinn?" The light grew nearer. "Tinn!"

I'm here, Tinn tried to say. But his lungs, already exhausted with the effort of each shallow breath, had no energy to spare on speaking.

A candle flame danced into his eyesight, and behind it hung the blurry face of Evie Warner. Tinn's heart thudded in his chest, and he managed a wobbly smile. Evie was saying something else now. It sounded like a question, but her voice was muffled as if she were speaking through a pillow. *Such a pretty face*, thought Tinn. He should tell Evie how happy he was to see her face. But then her candle was going out again—or Tinn was. The cavern grew dimmer and dimmer. Tinn lay on his back in the cold as Evie knelt over him, and the world went gently black.

Fable screamed as the earth fell away beneath her feet.

A lantern spun past her. In front of her, she saw Annie Burton grab hold of one of the twins and then reach out a frantic hand for the other. "Tinn! Take my hand!" Annie was yelling.

Fable's own hands flapped frantically, searching for something, anything, to catch hold of—and then strong fingers gripped her arm and she heard her mother's voice cry out: "Gale!"

A burst of air swept around them, sending Fable's curls whipping across her face. Fable's mother could have felled a tree with the force of the wind at her command if she had been in the Wild Wood. The breeze that followed her voice now did little more than set them spinning in circles as they fell.

"Gale!" Raina cried again. "Gale!" Fable felt each burst of air rising, like great big bubbles. The currents slowed their fall by only the faintest degrees.

Fable took a deep breath. The next time her mother cried out, she joined her. "Gale!" The two of them shouted as one. This time, the burst of air slapped them backward. Fable could not see through her own hair, but she felt the hard ground crash into her shoulder as her mother's hand was whipped out of hers. They were suddenly tumbling down a narrow side tunnel. The Wild Wood would not have allowed its witches to be so abused—but the Wild Wood was far above them now.

When the world had stopped thundering like a freight train around Fable, she gingerly sat up. It was too dark to see anything. Her shoulder stung, but she could still lift her arm enough to clap her hands together in a spray of sparks. It was her weakest "slappy sparks" in a long time— but against the total darkness, the flash still illuminated a female figure just ahead of her in the tunnel.

"Mama?" she called, but the woman did not respond. Fable slapped her hands together again, and this time she concentrated and held on to one little ember with her mind, coaxing the timid thing to life. It glowed a weak orange. "Mama?" The tunnel in front of her held nothing but shadows.

"Nnngh."

Fable spun around. Her mother was behind her, pushing herself up to sitting, her back leaning against the smooth rocks.

"Mama!"

"I'm here." Raina stretched her neck this way and that, wincing slightly. "Are you all right?"

Fable did a silent inventory of her own injuries. Her shoulder was throbbing, but she could move it. The stinging and aches in her legs and arms told her she would be covered in fresh bruises by morning, but nothing had struck too deeply. "I'll be fine," she said. "You?"

Raina grunted in pain as she rose to standing, but she managed it. She rotated each ankle carefully and twisted her torso to the left and right. "Nothing that won't heal."

"What do we do now?" said Fable.

"We find the others," said Raina. "And then we get out of here." Gingerly, she reached a hand toward Fable's timid ember. It swelled to a flame for a second and then split into two, and Raina drew one of the lights toward herself. The fire bobbed obediently in front of her, making their shadows bounce to and fro on the walls behind them.

"What if we're too late?" whispered Fable. "What if the others—"

"There is no such thing, remember?" Raina leaned in close and looked her daughter squarely in the eyes.

Fable swallowed her panic and nodded.

"Good," said Raina. "Let's get moving."

Cole screamed, his feet sliding out from under him as the ground buckled and collapsed. He felt himself go weightless for just a moment, and then a hand grabbed his shirtfront and he was pulled into a bear hug that could only be his mother's.

The two of them fell together.

"Tinn! Take my hand!" he heard her yell, and one arm left his back for a moment as his mom reached for Tinn. A lantern spun freely in the air beside them for several seconds until it caught the side of the shaft and was snuffed. He felt his mother's arm slap back around him. Where was Tinn?

Cole clung to his mother as tightly as he could. He felt a jarring bump as her backpack scraped the wall, and then a lurch as they were spun off to one side by a gust of wind. They hurtled down another shaft.

Cole closed his eyes and buried his face in his mother's shoulder. She groaned and tightened her grip as they skidded along an uneven stone chute.

The tunnel curved left and right in the impenetrable gloom, rising and falling like a Coney Island thrill ride, until finally it leveled out long enough for them to slide to a stop. The echoes around him told Cole that they were in a cave with a low ceiling. Somewhere nearby, water dripped serenely in the perfect darkness.

His mother's arms did not loosen for several seconds.

"Mom?" Cole managed. "Are you okay?"

She took five or six deep breaths before she finally let go. "Where's Tinn?" she wheezed.

A thumping, shuffling clamor arose behind them, and before Cole could reply, someone else came tumbling down through the pitch-black tunnel, skidding to a stop close beside them.

"Tinn?" said Annie.

The groan that followed was not his brother's. "Nope," grunted Old Jim. "Ungh. What were you saying about not splitting up?"

Annie sat up shakily, and Cole heard her patting her pockets. "Hold on. I've got a candle. I just need to find my matches. Where are my matches? Ugh, the pack's torn wide open."

"Allow me," said a nasal voice Cole didn't recognize at all.

They fell silent.

Slow footsteps echoed in the chamber around them.

"Hello?" said Cole.

The footsteps neared.

"Who's there?"

The *scritch* of a match answered, and Cole squinted as a tiny flare burst to life in front of him.

"Hold still," the voice said.

Cole's eyes finally adjusted and found their focus on a figure. It was a man—male, anyway. He could not have been any taller than Cole, and he wore dirty gray workman's clothes that hung off him as if they had once belonged to a much larger man. On his head was perched a miner's

128

helmet, but the face beneath was all wrong. The ears that stuck out under the brim of the helmet were leathery and pointed, his eyes were beads of glistening black and spaced far apart, and his nose was pushed up like a cave bat's. He smiled in a manner that might have been reassuring if it had not come from a mouth that was unsettlingly wide.

"You," said the creature, "are out of your depth."

FIFTEEN

THE STRANGE FIGURE LEANED DOWN AND touched his match to the candle still clutched in Annie's hand. The wick flickered and caught, and the darkness ebbed back a few more feet. Illumination did nothing to soften the stranger's features. He stood slightly hunched, holding on to a knotty walking stick. The candle's reflection bobbed in his glossy black eyes.

"That's better, isn't it?" He shook out the match and flicked it over his shoulder.

Annie managed to keep the candle steady, but her eyes were fixed on the stranger. "Who are you?"

"Nobody special," he answered, leaning on the stick. It

looked like a thick tree root and bent ever so slightly under his weight.

"You're a Tommyknocker, aren't you?" said Cole. "I've heard knockers dress like miners."

The figure shrugged. "*I've* heard that humans dress like delvers."

"Knockers aren't bad." Old Jim cleared his throat. "They make sounds to warn miners before cave-ins. Even help them find their way if they get lost. That true? Is that what you are?"

The figure tilted his head this way and that as he considered. "If you like," he said. "I do what I please. Others do what they please. You can call me Tommy, if it pleases you."

"We need help," said Annie. "I need to find my son and the rest of our friends."

"More of you?" said Tommy, his wispy eyebrows rising.

"Seven, altogether," said Annie. "The tunnel collapsed beneath us and we fell down different paths."

"So . . . not so *all together*," Tommy said.

"Will you help us find them?" Annie pressed.

The figure eyed the battered trio. He fiddled with a slim cord around his neck. "Might," he said simply. Then his eyes caught something on the floor beside Cole. "What's this?" He reached out with his walking stick and poked a slim gray disc. Cole patted his pockets as Tommy flipped the pendant over with a second jab to reveal the carving on the other side.

"That's mine," said Cole.

Tommy's beady eyes widened a fraction, then flicked to Cole and back to the pendant. His wide mouth tightened. "Is it?"

"It must have fallen out of my pocket when we hit the ground." Cole knelt and scooped up the disc. "It's why we're down here," he said, rubbing the familiar etching with his thumb. "Do you know what it means?"

Tommy gripped the gnarled root tightly in both hands. His eyes narrowed, his knees bent, and his muscles tensed.

"Whoa, now," said Old Jim.

"Wait! He doesn't mean any harm," Annie said, pushing herself upright clumsily.

Tommy lunged forward with a shriek and swung the knobby stick over his head like a cudgel. Cole leapt backward—but he needn't have dodged. Tommy's strike swung nowhere near him. It cracked off the stony ground behind him, narrowly missing a wiry creature who squealed in protest as it skittered away.

"Go on, then!" Tommy shouted after it. "Get! Shoo!"

The animal clambered halfway up the wall before turning to hiss angrily. It looked like something between an opossum and a monkey. Tommy raised the stick a second time, and the creature burrowed straight into the solid stones and disappeared with a *blip* like a drop of rain in a water barrel. Cole blinked. Where the thing had vanished, there remained not so much as a scratch in the surface of the sheer rock face.

"What on earth was that?" Annie said.

"Filthy kobold," Tommy muttered. "Nasty things. Usually they know better than to—" He sniffed experimentally, then faced the humans again with his mouth in a frown and one brow raised. "What did you bring?"

"What in Sam Hill are you talking about?" said Old Jim.

"We are *not* in Sam Hill," Tommy said, rounding on Old Jim. "We are in the Tenth Tier of the Elder Pass, and if there's *one* stinky kobold swimming in the sediment around us, then there are bound to be dozens more not far off. Kobolds can smell through solid bedrock—so . . . what did you bring?"

"I had sandwiches in my pack," said Annie. "That's probably it."

Tommy waved her off. "They're kobolds, not raccoons."

"I have some jerky in my pocket," said Cole.

"Meat?" The knocker looked at Cole as if he had just suggested kobolds might eat rainbows. He turned to Old Jim. "You. What did you bring?"

"Hm. Garlic?" said Old Jim, taking a bulb from his vest. "And some mustard seed and—let's see—my niece picked some fresh bitterwort." A handful of slightly crushed flowers slipped from his grip as he rooted through the pockets. Cole leaned down and picked them up.

Tommy shook his head and *tut-tut-tutted*. "We're talking about *kobolds*. Don't you three know anything? Rich metals? Gold rings? Silver brooches?"

"I got some silver," said Old Jim. He dug a little pendant from one of the pouches. It was no larger than a nickel. "Medal of Saint Christopher."

"That." Tommy nodded. "Leave it behind."

Old Jim's brow crinkled. "A Saint Christopher medal protects travelers from harm," he said.

"Not down here it doesn't," said Tommy. "Down here, precious metals attract pests, and pests cause plenty of harm. Toss it."

Old Jim took a step toward him, watching the odd little figure through narrow eyes. "I've also heard that *evil spirits* can't stand to be close to holy silver." He turned the medal over between his thumb and forefinger. "They say it burns their skin like fire." He held it out for Tommy to take it. "You're awfully keen to be rid of it. Why don't *you* toss it?"

Tommy stared flatly at Old Jim for several seconds and then took the coin in his bare palm, where it neither sizzled nor glowed red-hot. Tommy rolled his eyes. "Satisfied? You really *do* need my help, don't you?" He flicked the coin unceremoniously down a dark corridor like it was a spent cigarette butt. Its tinkle echoed through the tunnel and was quickly followed by the *scratch scratch* of talons on stone. Tommy's nose wrinkled as he eyed the passageway. "Keep it, you little monsters!" he called into the gloom.

"So?" said Cole. "Does that mean you'll help us?"

Tommy fiddled with the cord around his neck as he regarded the three of them. "Might," he said again. "Could help you find your way out." He tilted his head to one side, weighing the option. "Could help you find your friends." His head wobbled to the other side. "Could help you find your father. Lots of ways to help."

A tingle rippled up Cole's spine. "I never said we were looking for my father."

Tommy's beady eyes glinted in the candlelight. He pulled the cord around his neck up until it revealed from within his dusty clothes a disc about as wide as his palm hanging from the end. The disc spun gently, catching the light, revealing fine etching on one side. Cole's breath caught in his throat. He held a matching talisman in his hand.

"Lucky guess," said Tommy.

SIXTEEN

FABLE'S ARM FELT WARM AS SHE CONCENTRATED
on the hovering flame in front of her. It was not the heat
of the fire—the wavering orb of light at her fingertips was
no brighter than a match head—it was the prickling heat
of sustaining the magic for so long. It rippled through her
veins and pulsed with her heartbeat. The glow flickered
and dimmed, nearly going out more than once, but Fable
had practiced this spell a thousand times. If she let it flare
up too hot, it would burn itself out. Let it get too cool and
it would fizzle to nothing. The trick, like every other lesson her mother had drilled into her for her entire life, was
control.

Unlike in their lessons, this time her mother seemed to be having as much trouble controlling the spell as Fable did. A few paces ahead, the tunnel went dark again as her mother's flame sputtered and died to a floating ember. For the dozenth time, Raina stopped walking and concentrated on the light, coaxing it slowly back to life.

Fable took the opportunity to switch hands. She leaned against the cool stone wall and took a deep breath. They had been walking through narrow passages for what felt like hours, and they still had not seen any sign of the twins or Evie or the other grown-ups.

Fable sighed and watched the firelight bounce along the side of the tunnel. It made the rocks look almost alive, the way their shadows jittered and shook with each pulse of the flame. One smooth stone seemed to be wobbling more than the rest, and Fable held the flame higher to get a better look. It rippled like water in a heavy breeze, and then suddenly Fable was staring at a face with big, dark eyes and bristly whiskers.

She blinked.

The face blinked back.

"Uh. Hi," whispered Fable.

The face ducked back inside the rock and vanished.

"Come on," called Fable's mother, her flame alight once more. "We need to keep moving." She pressed forward, following the corridor as it sloped gradually up and to the left.

Fable ran a hand along the smooth stone in front of her. It was as solid as—well—a rock. There was no sign of any creature.

"I'm coming!" she called.

She continued to peer back over her shoulder as she rounded the corner. She could have sworn she heard the skittering of claws, like a squirrel clambering over a boulder. She squinted into the darkness for several seconds, but she could not see anything behind her.

Finally she turned her attention forward again.

The tunnel was dark.

"Mama?" she called. She willed her flame a little brighter. "Mama?"

The corridor split into two.

"This way!" her mother's voice echoed from the path on the left. Or was it the right?

This way, this way, this way! The echoes bounced all around the dark tunnel, but Fable was pretty sure they had started on the left.

"Coming!" Fable peered down the corridor. Yes—she could just make out her mother's silhouette in the darkness ahead. Her fire must have gone out again already. Her mother's magic was not working right at all down here.

Fable hurried to catch up.

"There was *something* skittery in the rocks back there," she said as she neared. "It looked sorta like a possum with huge eyes, but then it . . ." Fable's voice trailed off. Something was wrong. Her mother's cloak was wrapped too tightly around her shoulders. It hugged her frame more like a fitted dress than a furry bearskin, making her look too slender and too tall. "Mama?"

Her mother turned to face her.

No. No she didn't. Fable's heart pounded and the flame at her fingertips flared as the realization slammed into her—this was *not* her mother.

The woman's complexion was so pale, it bled into the gray of the cave around her. She had jet-black hair pulled back tightly on her head, and her high-collared dress was like velvety ash. She regarded Fable with an icy stare. The earth moved around the woman's feet, and a dozen dark, glossy eyes caught the firelight—more of the skittering rock creatures. Possum was a good comparison, except that their faces were flatter, more like primates, and their mouths were too big. Bristly fur melted into stones as the creatures scurried over one another, surrounding the woman's feet. The face Fable had seen poking out of the rocks back in the tunnel had seemed almost cute—like an ugly ferret or a baby gremlin. Now that she could see them out in the open, she wasn't sure *cute* was the right word for whatever these were. One of them hissed, baring too many teeth in its wide mouth, and then it clambered up the front of the woman's skirt.

The woman reached down without taking her eyes off Fable and scooped the feral creature up in one arm like a house cat. She stroked its coarse fur with her other hand while it continued to bare its teeth at Fable.

"Hello, little girl," said the woman. Something about the way she said the words *little girl* made the hair on Fable's neck stand on end. "You seem to have taken a bad turn."

"Don't hurt me," said Fable.

"Was that a *command?*" The woman turned to the creature on her arm as if the wiry rodent could confirm her suspicions. It squeaked. "Yes, I do believe the beastly thing just issued a command," said the woman. "To *me!*" She turned back to Fable. "The thing about commands," she said coldly, "is that when I am given them, I have this terrible urge to do the opposite." She let her final word hang in the air, its echo hissing in Fable's ears.

"My mama's the Queen of the Deep Dark," said Fable, trying to sound confident. The light in front of her flickered, thrumming weakly with each beat of her pounding heart. "Everybody's heard of her."

"Is she really?" The woman's expression did not change, but she leaned in so close Fable could feel the stranger's breath on her cheek. "Well, then. I shall endeavor to remind myself to curtsy when we meet." She did not raise her voice in the slightest, but the echo of her words still whispered back and forth around them in the cavern. The woman stood up straight, not taking her eyes from Fable. "You have ventured into my domain—*deeper* and *darker* than any lands over which your royal mother might claim dominion. Would you continue to delve? Do you seek the *deepest*? The *darkest*?"

Fable swallowed.

"Be careful, child." The woman's voice was venom, and her gaze bored into Fable like a knife tip. "Or you might be unfortunate enough to find *precisely* what you seek."

A roar erupted behind Fable and shook the dust from the ceiling. The stranger's eyes widened in surprise. In her bear form, Raina pounded forward.

The stranger took a step back, away from the rapidly approaching wall of teeth and claws and fur, until she was pressed against the side of the tunnel. The bristly creatures at her feet screeched and chittered. Raina was nearly upon her when, with a sound like old pipes tapping, the air around the woman rippled and she sank into solid stone, pets and all.

Raina raked her claws against the rocks where they had vanished, but the tunnel wall was unyielding. She snarled in frustration.

"I would not treat these hallowed passageways so shamefully," came an indignant voice from somewhere behind Fable and Raina.

With some difficulty in the tight space, Raina turned around. The stranger's pallid features slid up from the rocks on the opposite side of the tunnel like a diver emerging from the water.

The bear chuffed and narrowed her eyes.

"These tunnels have borne the tides of time for longer than any of you have walked the earth above them—but they will still collapse on top of those careless enough to test them." The woman stepped free of the rocks and stood, placidly petting the wiry gray creature still perched on the arm of her dress.

The bear's head lifted until it was nearly touching the ceiling, and then, with a swooping motion, Raina was human again, lowering the hood of her furry cloak. Her eyes remained locked on the stranger.

The pale woman's lips turned up in the slightest hint of a smile. The creature on her arm made a raspy purring sound as she stroked its ears. "Ah," she said. "I take it I am in the presence of royalty. What a treat." Her voice remained flat. "I've always wondered: is it true what they say about royal blood being blue?"

"You are in the presence of a *mother*," Raina growled. "Threaten my daughter again, and it won't be *my* blood you'll need to worry about."

"I do not threaten, *Your Majesty*." The woman's voice dripped with mock decorum. "But I do give warnings. You would be ill-advised to ignore them."

"Who are you?" Raina demanded.

"Oh, *now* she wants to know my name? I'm learning so much about queens," said the woman, talking more to the creature on her arm than to either of them. "See, I would have thought introductions would come *before* attacks, silly me. Etiquette is such a funny thing." She lifted her wrist up to her shoulder, and the bristly creature scampered off her arm and made itself comfortable curled up behind her neck. The woman raised her chin to meet Raina's gaze. "I am the one they call Gruvrået."

Raina blinked.

"Did she say Grew Fruit?" whispered Fable.

The woman's cheeks flushed and her jaw tightened. "It is unwise to mock a rået," she growled through clenched teeth.

"I'm not making fun," said Fable. "I just don't know what that word is. There's loads of stuff I don't know. It

143

sounds like you said *root*. And that's probably not what you said, but a root would be a pretty neat thing to be."

The woman's brow remained tightly creased as she regarded Fable.

"Roots are good," Fable explained. "They're sturdy, like anchors, and they hold together the whole ground, so we don't get landslides or erosion. Plus they're how all the living stuff keeps living. We don't usually think about roots very much because we can't see them under the ground— but basically everything in the whole world depends on them being there."

The woman shook her head, but the corner of her lip had curled up in a faint smile. "I have been called many things by many people. I am the Mistress of the Mines, the Lady of the Mountain. But you"—she nodded to Fable— "you may call me Madam Root."

"I *have* heard of you," said Raina. "The fair folk told me stories when I was a little girl. There were once guardian spirits, rå, who lived long before the split between fairies and humankind. They were a noble race, wardens of the earth who refused to leave their posts on this side of the veil when the world was divided."

The gray woman—Madam Root—bowed her head. "Then we are not entirely forgotten. This is good. What else do the stories say?"

144

"That the rå vanished, long ago," said Raina. "That, when magic left the earthly world, all the beings of raw magic either died off or . . . *changed*. Some say they became one with the rivers and the rocks and the wind." She took a deep breath. "If you truly *are* a rået—you should not exist."

Madam Root was silent. Her eyes stared, unfocused, into the darkness for several long seconds.

"I'm sorry—" Raina began.

"No. You are wrong." Madam Root snapped back to the moment, fixing her gaze on Raina. "And you are trespassing."

Raina did not blink. "We are. But it is necessary."

"Necessary? Is the world above not big enough for you? Must you expand your glorious kingdom to the very center of the earth?"

"I do not have a *glorious kingdom*, I have a *forest*," Raina answered, and Fable recognized her mother's witchy voice. It was the voice her mother used when she had to be the Queen of the Deep Dark for real, a voice that could silence quarreling pixies and subdue rebellious hobs—it was a voice sharpened to a razor edge. "I also have a duty," Raina continued, "to protect those who live within my lands." She took a step forward. "Including those who have been *stolen* from them."

"Is that so?" Madam Root raised an eyebrow.

The two eyed each other appraisingly. It was like watching fencers circling before a duel. If they had been lionesses, their tails would have been twitching.

"What exactly do you know about the stolen?" said Madam Root.

"I know that people and creatures have been taken from aboveground and kept here, below," said Raina, "in what you have made perfectly clear is *your* domain. I do not yet know the reason, but I will. Is their capture your doing?"

"Hmh." Madam Root made a noise that might have been a laugh. "*My doing* is none of your concern, wood witch," she said. "I have been *doing* since before the oldest tree in your forest was even a seed, and I will continue to *do* with or without your leave. You will get nothing back. I promise you that. Dig too deeply, and you will lose even more." She paused. "But I am curious. You came all this way for stolen souls. Did you intend to bargain with me for their return? Or threaten me until I release them?"

"Neither would do me any good, would it?" answered Raina.

Madam Root did not reply.

"No, I think not." Raina answered her own question, and her shoulders relaxed. "Because you did not take them."

Madam Root's head cocked to one side. "And how could you possibly be so sure of that?"

"You would be happy to let me think that you did," said Raina. The deadly edge was gradually fading from her voice, like a hound's hackles slowly lowering. In its place, Fable could detect just a hint of amusement in her mother's cadence. "You would be happy to let me think you were a thief and a killer. To let me hate you. To let me fear you." Raina regarded Madam Root thoughtfully. "Fear would serve its purpose. Fear is power, of a sort."

The little creature on Madam Root's shoulder poked its head up and blinked two overlarge eyes at Raina.

"They used to whisper my name," the woman said. "When their lanterns sputtered and the cold crept over them." She stroked the little creature's chin. "And they left offerings. If they heard my warning taps and cleared out before a collapse, or if the stone gave way and revealed a rich vein—they would leave me gifts. Human coins. Polished stones. My sweet kobolds used to delight in finding them. I loved to see them happy, the wee things." The creature on her shoulder was purring. "But over time, their gifts came less often. They took more and left less. Do you know how long it has been since I heard any of my titles on a human tongue?"

"They stopped believing in you."

"And yet I am still here."

"It's about stories," said Raina, gently. "They *need* the stories. I have a bit of experience with that myself. I would be happy to give you a few suggestions." Madam Root raised her eyes warily. "Have you considered a career as a terrifying hag?" asked Raina. "It can be surprisingly rewarding."

"You mock me."

"Do I look like I'm laughing? You could be the most feared force in the underground."

Madam Root shook her head. "I do not need their fear. But it would be nice to have their respect back."

Raina leaned back and heaved a sigh. "Fear is easier. But when all this is over, I will see what I can do."

"Why?"

Raina straightened. "Because," she said with authority, "we are queens."

"I am not a queen."

"Aren't you, now?"

"If ever I had a right to that title, that time is far behind me."

"Keep telling yourself that, and you will allow *them* to believe it," Raina said. "Let idiot men fear you or let them forget you—their opinions make you no less a queen."

Madam Root regarded Raina for several seconds. "Queens have power," she said. "No power in the earth will bring back what I have lost." She drew a deep breath, and her shoulders sagged within her ashen gown. Her face was a mix of fury and frustration and . . . something else. Fable couldn't quite place it. Something *sad*.

"What did you lose?" said Fable.

Madam Root finally broke eye contact with Raina, letting her gaze drift upward. "Not as much as *you* are going to lose," she said. She said it not with venom, but with a sort of chilly, dreadful certainty.

An icy breeze howled through the cavern, sending shivers up Fable's neck. With a muffled *fizz*, the orb of light at her fingertips fell dark, and the cave went black.

SEVENTEEN

TINN OPENED HIS EYES. A BLURRY LIGHT FLOATED in front of him. He blinked, trying to focus. Something was dragging him along the rocky ground by one foot. Instinctively he tugged it back.

"Tinn?" said Evie, startled. She turned, and a patch of candlelight illuminated her face. "Tinn! Oh, thank goodness! I'm really sorry about bonking your head. It's hard to navigate down here."

"My head?" Tinn mumbled.

"Nothing," said Evie. "You probably bumped it during the fall, and not while I was pulling you across the floor."

Tinn pushed himself up to sitting. It took tremendous effort, like his body was made of lead. "Ugh. I feel like I got run over by a train. How'd you make it down here without getting hurt?"

"Oh, I got plenty hurt. Check out my arms." Evie pulled up her sleeves. Tinn was used to counting bruises after an especially rocky adventure, but it would have been easier to count the rare patches of Evie's arms that were *not* bruised. "Pretty nasty cut on my knee, too," she said. "And a lump on the back of my head that's gonna smart tomorrow. But it could be a lot worse."

"Dang. You're taking it well. You don't even seem sore."

Evie shrugged. "I'm good at being sore."

Tinn tilted his head. He still felt foggy, and he wasn't sure if she was joking or not.

"I'm a foot shorter than everybody I hang out with, and my joints are as bad as Uncle Jim's," said Evie. "If I stopped moving every time I was sore, I'd never get anything done."

"Huh." Tinn nodded. "Well, I'm definitely *not* good at being sore—not *this* sore, anyway. My whole body hurts."

"Think you can stand?"

"I'll give it a try."

With Evie's help, Tinn stood up. Pain rippled through his limbs. His ankle had taken a bad hit on the way down, and it throbbed in rhythm with his heartbeat—but at least he could put weight on it. He looked around as he tested out each muscle carefully. By the light of Evie's candle, he could see that the cavern was huge. The walls sloped outward as they rose, making it feel like they were stuck in the bottom of a giant bowl, or perhaps on the inside of an enormous globe. He couldn't see the ceiling properly—the candlelight only pushed back the gloom so far—but he guessed it was at least a hundred feet above them.

"We popped out up there," Evie said, pointing at a spot high on the wall behind him. "And sorta slid and rolled down the slope. It wasn't exactly smooth, and it tore up my vest on one side so I lost half of my stuff, but I'm still counting it as lucky."

"Didn't feel especially lucky."

"Yeah, well. Imagine if the shaft had opened up right in the middle and dropped us straight down, instead of along the slope," she said. She made a low whistle as her eyes traced an imaginary descent from the ceiling to the rocky floor. "Splat."

"Fair enough," said Tinn. "So how do we get out?"

"Climbing back the way we came is no good," she said. "I tried. A bunch of times. It just gets too steep and there's no good footholds. There are a couple of tunnels over on that side of the cave, though. The one on the right zigzags a bunch and gets narrower after a few minutes, but the one on the left feels like it slopes up bit by bit. I think that's our best bet."

"How long have I been out?" Tinn shook his head.

"I've been through two candles," answered Evie. "So . . . an hour at least?"

"How many candles do we have left?"

Evie swallowed. She held up the stub still flickering in her hand. "About a half?"

Tinn took a deep breath. "Tunnel on the left it is."

Evie held the candle aloft as they walked, but still, Tinn found himself stumbling and knocking his already abused head against the rocks. He needed better eyes if he was going to get through this without pummeling himself senseless.

Better eyes. Tinn felt like an idiot—he could *do* that! What was the point of being a changeling if he didn't use his powers when he needed them?

He concentrated as they moved forward, imagining his own eyes taking on the narrow slits of a cat's. He felt the familiar warm tingle of transformation bouncing around his skull for a moment, and then gradually the darkness shifted. It worked! The tunnel did not become less dark, exactly, but the shadows gained distinction. He could make out Evie's shoulders and the faint light catching her hair. He could see the moisture on the rocks and the curve of the tunnel up ahead. Tinn allowed himself a smile.

His moment of good cheer fell away as the echoes of a piteous cry drifted toward them out of the darkness. Tinn froze. He met Evie's nervous glance, and the two of them held perfectly still as they listened. In the distance, they could make out the word *"Please,"* and then another word was cut short by a howl of pain.

"The other tunnel is starting to sound pretty good," Tinn murmured.

Evie glanced at what was left of her candle and then turned her face toward the source of the noise. "The other tunnel could lead to nothing," she whispered. "This one definitely leads to something."

Tinn steeled his jaw and nodded. "Starting to really wish I had taken Kull up on that sneaking lesson," he murmured. Together, they crept around the next bend and the next, until they could make out a faint light coming from up ahead. Muffled voices bounced around the corner.

". . . only unconscious," one of them was saying.

"That's fine. I hate when they go on and on anyway."

Evie snuffed out the candle and tucked the stub back into one of the pouches on her vest. Breathlessly, the two of them peeked around the edge of the last turn.

Torchlight flooded the scene before them. A body lay slumped on the ground, small, lumpy, and clad in dirty scraps. It looked to Tinn like a hob—harmless forest folk. He clenched his fists. Hobs were tactless and occasionally greedy, but they would never harm a soul. They didn't even have sharp fangs or claws or any natural advantages in a fight.

Three figures stood over the hob, all clad in matching dusty red robes. Their faces were inhuman, but Tinn couldn't place their species—their heads were too thick to be elfin and too slight to be trolls. They had beady eyes and long, leathery ears, and their noses were squashed up against their faces like they had run headlong into a wall too many times. One of them wore a leather cap, but the other two had wiry hair brushed straight back on their heads.

The closest robed figure was turned away from Tinn and Evie, and they could clearly see a symbol stitched into the back of his garments in fiery orange thread.

Evie nudged Tinn. The sigil was a circular design like a tree with a rounded top—identical to the one Cole had been carrying around for weeks—except this version was encompassed by a serpent. The orange thread caught the firelight in flashes and glimmers, as if the whole design were made of liquid fire.

"Loyal acolytes," a voice boomed from just up the passageway. "Is the offering prepared?" The robed figures all straightened and snapped to attention.

"Yes, Low Priest," the one with his back to Tinn and Evie replied. "She was moaning terribly about the honor she is to receive, so we told her to be quiet."

The Low Priest stepped slowly into view. He was clad like the others, but the fabric of his robes almost seemed to glow and shift like liquid magma, and it bore none of the dust and soot that coated the others'. Around his neck hung a polished stone pendant, the familiar rounded-tree sigil etched on its surface.

"She didn't listen the first time," said the acolyte in the leather cap. His tiny, dark eyes glinted in the torchlight. "So we told her more *firmly* the second time."

At their feet, the unfortunate hob chose this moment to groan and rouse herself. "Unngh."

A shadow rippled behind the Low Priest, and a chilly tingle ran up Tinn's spine. The scar on the palm of his hand felt ice-cold.

I SMELL FEAR, said a voice that reverberated uncomfortably in Tinn's skull. He held his breath. The Thing did not tower over the acolytes as it would have in its former glory, but slunk along the ground like a hungry wolf. It was a shapeless mass of dripping shadows, its hide constantly shifting like the swirling ashes of a fire. It clearly had not returned to its full power since their last encounter, but there was no doubt this was the same monster that had nearly consumed Tinn in the heart of the Wild Wood.

The acolytes eyed the Thing warily as it approached the hob.

HELLO, LITTLE HOB, said the Thing. YOU ARE A LONG WAY FROM HOME.

Tinn's knees bent and his whole body tensed. He couldn't let the Thing kill that helpless creature. Evie gripped his arm firmly. "No," she whispered. "It's too dangerous."

"G-g-go away!" stammered the hob, finally finding consciousness in time to clumsily tumble backward away from the Thing, eyes suddenly wide with terror.

A tendril of shadows swept behind the frightened creature, catching her before her back could hit the ground. The hob cringed as the darkness touched her skin. Her eyes clenched shut and she began to whimper.

One of the wiry-haired acolytes took a half step backward, his expression visibly disgusted. "What is the darkling doing?" he asked.

"Have you never seen the darkling at work, Korvum?" The Low Priest kept his eyes on the Thing as he answered. "What a treat for you, then. Our esteemed guest is feeding on the emotions of this evening's offering, drinking the creature's fear and panic. In time, the simple beast will feel nothing at all."

"Is that . . . wise?" Korvum asked. He pulled his eyes away from the Thing and turned back to the Low Priest. "That is, shouldn't the Ancient One receive the whole of the gift? Is it not wrong to offer a weakened sacrifice?"

The Low Priest took slow steps toward Korvum, and the other acolytes backed away, averting their eyes.

"I-I'm sorry, Low Priest," Korvum stammered. "I should not have questioned your will."

"No. It is good," said the Low Priest. "You wish only the best for the Ancient One. It is right to be generous to our once and future master. Your generosity will be remembered."

"Th-thank you, Low Priest."

The priest turned to the Thing. "Darkling, leave the tribute."

The Thing halted and turned what might have been a head toward the Low Priest. The hob took a gasping breath, like it had just emerged from underwater.

I EXERCISE RESTRAINT, hissed the Thing. THERE WILL STILL BE PLENTY OF MARROW LEFT IN THE BONES.

"I said leave it."

The Thing's shadows rippled with its displeasure. The tendrils released the pathetic hob, coils of darkness crawling back around the Thing like a swarm of bees returning to the hive. For a moment Tinn wondered if the priest was about to become its next meal.

"Do not fret," the Low Priest added. "You will not go hungry. I have promised you your strength, after all, and Acolyte Korvum has kindly offered himself, that you might feast without such cumbersome restraint."

The acolyte's eyes widened, and his skin lost what little color it had.

"He is," the priest added, "*very* generous."

"Low Priest, wait!" But Korvum's plea was cut short as watery darkness whipped around the acolyte and enveloped him. The hob dragged herself to the wall as the dark shape that had once been Korvum sank to his knees.

Tinn could not watch. He pressed his back to the stones and closed his eyes. The scar on his palm surged with pain, and he concentrated on breathing evenly to keep from passing out. When he dared glance back, the Thing's shadows were rippling away from a pile of red robes and ashen bones.

The Thing swelled, its darkness looking ever so slightly more solid.

"Would either of you care to voice any concerns?" the Low Priest asked. The remaining acolytes shook their heads. "Excellent. Then let us proceed to the ritual. Bring the hob."

The Thing raised its head, turning this way and that like a hound on the scent. THAT SMELL.

The Low Priest glanced down at the cowering hob. "Has it soiled itself? The last one made such a mess."

IT IS NOT THE HOB.

The pain in Tinn's hand was becoming unbearable. He hugged it to his chest. This was bad. This was very bad. His heart thudded in his ears. With his free hand he grabbed Evie's arm and silently urged her back, behind him.

I KNOW THAT SMELL. The Thing finally fixed on their direction. Its shadows melted and re-formed, melted and re-formed, shifting closer and closer.

Tinn and Evie pressed back as quietly as they could. Every scuff of a shoe against the stone sounded like an alarm bell. Tinn wanted so badly to run, to barrel down the passageway. But there was no outrunning the Thing. There was only hoping it wouldn't . . .

The Thing slid around the corner directly in front of him. Tinn felt numb. It was so close, Tinn could have reached out and touched it—but then it stopped. The Thing's shadows were just as Tinn remembered them, swirling slivers of ice and smoke and ink, dripping and weaving through the air. One could almost imagine that the shadows were a dark veil draped over some wild beast. Through the darkness, Tinn could almost make out the shape at the heart of the Thing. In the middle of the hateful, horrible monster was a terrified scrap of a real, solid, living creature. It was still in there, somewhere. Tinn had seen it before, just once.

Tinn felt faint. The Thing stared straight at him for several seconds, breathed him in, then made a noise like a contented sigh. Tinn's mind was racing. Fight? Run? Stand his ground? He thought he just might be able to endure whatever torment the horrible villain had prepared for him if it meant knowing that Evie could escape. And then the Thing did something Tinn was not prepared for.

It left.

As fluidly as they had found him, the Thing's shadows slipped back around the bend in the corridor.

IT IS NOTHING, they heard its haunting voice say. VERMIN.

Tinn let out the breath that was beginning to burn in his chest. What had just happened? The Thing *had* him. Had he turned invisible? He glanced down—no—still the same bruised elbows and scraped knees, fully visible. Even if he had vanished, the Thing had smelled him. It *knew* him. What was it up to?

"Kobolds," said one of the acolytes. "These paths are crawling with them."

YES, said the Thing.

"Then let us proceed to the Low Altar," said the priest. "There will not be many more sacrifices before the great awakening."

The sound of footsteps and the whimpering of the hob grew quieter and quieter as they withdrew.

"Come on," whispered Evie. "We need to follow them. They're going to kill that hob."

"Yeah," said Tinn. "They are. And I don't want that to happen any more than you do, but us getting killed alongside her won't make her any less dead. We need to get out of here."

"Do you know what the *Ancient One* is?" said Evie.

"No," said Tinn. "Some creepy cult thing."

"Okay, how about the *great awakening?*"

"I don't know."

"Wouldn't you like to?"

"Not particularly. I'd like to be not buried in a hole with monsters."

Evie crossed her arms. "Those creeps are paying tribute to something even scarier than that shadow monster, and they're getting ready for something *huge* to happen. I'd rather find out what it is and how to stop it than find my

162

way back to the surface and be stuck wondering when it's going to pop out of the ground beneath my feet. I'm going to follow them."

Tinn shook his head. "You're going to get caught."

Evie considered this for a moment. "Yeah," she said. "I am." In the dark, Tinn could almost believe he saw her lips turn up in a smile.

EIGHTEEN

Cole, Annie, and old Jim followed Tommy through one narrow passage after another. "What does the symbol mean?" asked Cole for the dozenth time.

"You'll see for yourself," Tommy answered patiently. "It's not far now."

"Why a tree?" Cole pressed. "Is it a nature thing?"

"Tree?" Tommy glanced back to Cole. He narrowed his eyes. "Not a tree."

"Then what is it?"

"It's . . . the world."

"How is it the world?"

Tommy walked a few more paces before he turned and faced Cole. He held up his own sigil and ran a slim finger along the curve at the top. "Your home," he said. "Above." He pointed toward the middle of the symbol—to what Cole had considered the branches. "Us. Now." He pointed at the bottom—to what Cole had seen as the base of the trunk. "The pillar."

Cole stared at the etching. "Oh! So the lines sticking out are like tunnels, and there's one big tunnel going right down to the bottom?"

"Not exactly," said Tommy, continuing through the underground pathway again. "Those lines aren't the *empty bits*, they're the *solid bits*. Support columns."

"You're saying the surface world—where we live—is like a shell resting on a big, empty earth?" said Cole. "And the whole thing is held up by just one column?"

Tommy nodded. "More or less," he said.

"That's nonsense," said Annie. "The earth isn't hollow."

"Not the *whole* earth," said Tommy. "Just our bit. Almost there."

"Miners dig down all the time," said Annie. "We would know if the ground beneath us was hollow."

Tommy chuckled. "*Delvers* dig. Miners scratch. We listen to them scratch, scratch, scratching, all the time. Do you know how deep the deepest tunnels at your Echo Point run?"

"Hundreds of feet down," said Annie. "My husband worked in those mines."

Tommy smirked. "Mm. Exactly. Hundreds of feet. Maybe a whole mile? Hm? Your husband scratched a little deeper than a few hundred feet." He rounded a corner, and light began to filter along the corridor. "Wanna see what he found?"

They followed Tommy around the bend, and the space suddenly yawned open before them.

"Whoa," breathed Cole.

Annie put a hand on his shoulder, unable to find words for what she was seeing.

"Sweet sassy molasses," Old Jim mumbled.

Cole had only ever seen the Grand Canyon in photographs at school, but he imagined standing on its ledge would feel a lot like looking down into these mind-boggling depths. The entire town of Endsborough could have fit between them and the far side of the cave—a distance Cole could only barely make out, thanks to a faint reddish glow lighting the fog that appeared to be thousands of feet beneath them. It was anyone's guess how far below the fog the pit continued to descend. Cole glanced up.

The cave continued upward another thousand feet at least. It hurt his eyes to try to make out any details in the dim distance.

In the center of it all, running from the shadowy heights of the vaulted ceiling to the fathomless depths of the cloudy floor, was a thick column of deep gray stone. It was hard to comprehend the size of the pillar from so far away, but it had to be hundreds of feet around. Cole couldn't tell if it got thinner at the bottom or if that was just a trick of the perspective—either way, it made his stomach spin just looking at it. Massive marbled columns jutted out from the central pillar like support beams under a bridge.

"Okay," Annie managed. "You win. This part looks pretty hollow."

Tommy ignored her. A wide steel rod had been bolted to the wall beside him, running up into the shadowy heights above and down into the foggy distance far below. Next to this, a rusty chain hung from a series of pulleys and big, slowly turning cogs. Tommy began tugging the chain, and a muffled rattle echoed up.

Cole leaned his head out over the edge to peer down, and Annie instinctively tightened her grip on his shoulder. "What's below the clouds?" he asked.

"Answers," replied Tommy. He continued to pull on the chain. A metal cage about six feet tall was rattling upward on the other end.

"Straight answers?" asked Annie. "You keep giving us pieces. What *aren't* you telling us?"

Tommy did not stop hauling on the chain. The box had nearly reached their platform. "You ever ridden an elevator?" he asked. "Marvelous things, elevators. Gnomish design, this one, with some goblin craftsmanship. The thing about elevators, though, is that they only go two places. Up. Or down."

"Where are you taking us?" asked Annie.

"You tell me." Tommy locked his eyes on her. "You want to go up? Say the word. Sunlight and blue skies. Easy." He scratched behind his leathery ear. "But I'm pretty sure you're going to choose down."

"Why would we—"

"Because you're looking for the boy's father, and I can take you exactly where he went."

Annie fell silent as Tommy gave the chain a final tug. A brass cage with a door right in the middle hung in front of them, swaying slightly in space while the knocker secured its chain.

"I was there," said Tommy. "*He* chose *down*. How about you?"

Annie swayed a little, and Cole held her hand.

"I'm with you either way," said Old Jim. "What do you say?"

Cole looked at his mother. Her eyes were pained.

"Mom?" he whispered.

"We are going to find your brother," she said. "And our friends, and—Lord help me—your father, if he really is down there. But I need *you* to be safe, Cole." She shook her head. "I can handle losing my husband—I've done that before—but I *can't* lose you or Tinn. So if we're going to do this, I need you to promise me something."

"Of course."

"This isn't a game. We're not playing heroes. If things go badly, you run away, fast as you can. Do you understand?"

Cole nodded, earnestly. "I promise."

Annie took a deep breath. "Okay," she said. "Down."

Tommy opened the cage's door with a squeak. The elevator swung and creaked as they stepped inside.

"You sure this is safe?" said Old Jim.

"It was designed by gnomes," said Tommy, as if that sorted the matter neatly.

"Gnomes weigh a lot less than people do," Old Jim grumbled.

"It will hold your weight," Tommy assured him.

Once they were all inside, Tommy followed, clicking

the door shut and pulling a lever by his side. The box trembled, the gears on the wall above them clanked, and they were descending, slowly at first, then faster and faster. Cole's stomach felt woozy almost at once.

"It's easier if you focus on a single point," said Tommy, as if reading Cole's thoughts.

Cole stared at the base of the central pillar. It did look a bit like a tree, after all. How much was resting on that single trunk? What would happen to the world above if it were to crack or crumble? Somehow that line of thought only made his stomach turn in tighter knots.

The mist was drawing nearer. Tommy adjusted the lever and their descent slowed down a fraction. "How are there clouds underground?" asked Annie.

"Same reason there are clouds above." Tommy shrugged. "Moisture. Heat. Room to form. These clouds are special, though. They form from the waters of sacred underground springs."

The mist rose up to meet them now, and the world went white. It was warmer than Cole had expected, and the tiny droplets tickled his throat as he breathed them in.

"There are twin rivers that circle this whole place under the ground," Tommy went on. "Did you know? They open out above and feed a lot of the lakes and springs and swamplands in your Wild Wood."

Cole blinked, watching the mist spin and churn around them as they slipped through it. Something about the way it moved felt strangely familiar.

"The River Truth and the River Lies," Tommy said. "The old delvers found ways to use the waters from the River Truth. They drank it, brewed it in powerful teas, even diverted it over magma to form a vapor that would give them divine clarity. It's how they made their prophecies." He patted the flask on his hip. "Potent stuff."

They were in the thick of it now. Everything around them was white. Cole's head didn't feel very clear.

"Of course, later delvers found they could manipulate the River Lies, too. They spent decades getting the mixture just right. Mixed in all kinds of things. Lotus leaves, asphodel, finfolk weed . . . they developed the cloud layer you see today. Clever. And effective."

"Wait. You said swamplands. You mean the Oddmire?" Cole asked—or at least he meant to. What actually came out sounded droopy and wrong, like the words were melting as they left his lips. The Oddmire—that's what the swirling shapes reminded him of. They looked just like the mists hanging over the Oddmire. Only these ones came straight from the source, which meant . . . which meant . . . What did it mean? Cole's head felt as if the fog had rolled right through it and clouded up his whole brain.

Suddenly the strange clouds were above them and the elevator was slowing as it neared solid ground. Cole lifted his head and blinked. His body felt like it was made of taffy. Tommy was saying something again, but the words tumbled around in the air like addled butterflies.

Cole blinked again, and when he opened his eyes this time, the elevator had come to a complete stop. How long had they been stopped? The door was already open, and Tommy was helping Cole's mother out of the cage. Cole's fingers felt funny. He glanced down at his hands and saw that he was holding a fistful of crumpled yellow flowers. That was important for some reason. He had been about to . . . about to . . . what?

And then they were walking. How long had they been walking? Where was the elevator? Tommy's voice rang through the fog like a bell: "Follow me," he instructed, and those two words were everything Cole knew. He would follow Tommy. Following Tommy was the answer. Somewhere in the back of Cole's head, a different voice was also telling him to chew. Chew what? Chewing was *not* following Tommy. He needed to follow Tommy. But perhaps he could chew *and* follow at the same time.

He bit down experimentally, and a burst of bitterness flooded over his tongue. Cole grimaced. The flowers—

right—he had put them in his mouth. Why had he done that? He chewed the vile plant as he stumbled forward.

"New converts," said Tommy, ahead of them.

Cole forced his eyes to find focus. In front of him, his mother and Old Jim had stopped walking and were swaying on their feet as they waited. Two creatures in dark red robes stood in front of them, speaking to Tommy. Like Tommy, each of them had leathery skin and dark, beady eyes that sat on either side of a nose so flat it looked like it had been pressed up by a rolling pin.

"Three at once?" grunted one of the robed figures. "You trying to impress somebody?"

"These ones did the work for me," Tommy replied with a shrug. "You know the one who got away during that darkling mess a few months back?"

"The worm sneaking around in the unused passages?"

"Yeah. These ones are related to him. If we use them right, we might finally get a chance to flush him out. There are more of them, too, still lost in the tunnels. I'll track them down."

"I'd be quick about it," the second robed figure said. "The Low Priest is not happy that we still haven't caught the last one. The order are on their way to the altar right now with the latest tribute."

"*All* of them will be tributes, soon enough." Tommy turned back toward Cole and the grown-ups. "All right. Go with the nice acolytes," he said firmly.

His mother and Old Jim shuffled forward, their shoulders slumping like marionettes with broken strings as they plodded ahead.

"Wait," Cole groaned.

Tommy turned to look at him. "I said *go with them,*" Tommy repeated. The command pulled at Cole. It would be so easy to just do as he was told—but no. No, this was wrong. Cole resisted. He swallowed, feeling bitter herbs rush down his throat and bitter clarity rush over his mind.

"No!" he yelled. His own voice sounded hollow in his ears. "It's a trick! Mom! Snap out of it!"

His mother did not turn her head. Her feet shuffled along the rocks as she trudged forward.

"Mom! Mr. Warner! Wake up!"

"Seven sleeping hells, Tommy, how did you manage to botch a basic conversion?" the first acolyte snapped. "Shut that kid up before one of the Lowest hears him. It's nearly time for the offering! If he interrupts a sacrifice, the priest will make you *wish* it had been you they were feeding to the Ancient One."

"Mom!" Cole screamed. But it was no use. She couldn't seem to hear him.

"It's fine. I'll take care of him," Tommy grumbled, and stalked toward Cole. His fingers twitched as he rounded on the boy. Cole backed away. "Hold still, kid."

Tommy lunged, but Cole ducked out of the way at the last second. Tommy stumbled, but managed to catch his footing after a few steps. Cole spared a glance at his mother, but she just stood there, glassy-eyed. She had made him promise not to play the hero—not that it made it any easier. Cole swallowed hard. He would come back for them, but first, he would do as he had promised. He would *run* as fast as he could.

And so he did.

NINETEEN

BY THE TIME FABLE HAD REKINDLED HER SPARK, the mysterious Madam Root was gone and she and her mother found themselves alone again.

"We need to keep moving," Raina said. Fable stayed close behind her as they pressed onward.

Maintaining a glowing ball of flame was getting harder and harder. Using magic was like flexing a muscle—it might be easy enough to pick up a hefty rock, but it was something else entirely to hold that rock out at arm's length for hours on end. Fable's mental magic muscles felt like soggy bread, and her light pulsed and sputtered weakly. Her mother seemed to be having no better luck with her own. When her mother's went out, Fable put in extra effort to keep hers going, and when hers went out, her mother did the same.

It was hard to tell if they had made any progress upward at all, or if—as Fable silently suspected—they were actually sloping farther into the earth. The uneasiness only made it harder to focus on her flame, and for the dozenth time, she lost it. As luck would have it, her mother's light chose the same moment to expire, and they both drew to a halt as darkness swept over them again.

Fable sighed. "I'll start the next one," she said, and lifted her hands to clap out a new spark.

"Wait," her mother said. "Look. Do you see something?"

Fable squinted. Ahead of them, the faintest warm glow defined the opening to a tunnel ahead. With their fires lit, they might have missed it.

"Do you think it's sunlight?" Fable could not remember a time when she had been away from fresh air and the open sky for so long.

"I think it's *something*. Stay close to me."

They trod slowly toward the source of the glow. The light grew brighter around every turn they took, until soon they could make out waves and eddies of mist spilling around their feet. In the light of the eerie glow, the clouds of mist looked blood red.

"It smells . . . magicky," Fable said.

"*Magicky* is not a word," her mother answered.

"Well, that's what it smells like," Fable said.

"Yes." Raina crinkled her nose. "It does." It was a familiar magic, not entirely unlike the nature magic of the Wild Wood. But this was not the queen's magic. It would not obey her, as the forest did.

They trod a little deeper, and the billowing mist grew thicker. Now it reached Fable's knees, always moving, spinning, twisting. She reached down and drew her fingers through it, watching the particles churn at her touch. She didn't notice that her mother had stopped, and she plowed right into her back.

"What—"

"Listen," her mother whispered.

Fable went quiet.

Footsteps.

The two of them remained rooted to the spot, listening as the footsteps neared. Gradually, a shape appeared ahead of them. It was only a dark lump in the fog at first, but the figure sharpened as it emerged from the cloud with the *slap, slap* of bare feet on the stones. Soon they could see that it was a bald, greenish creature, no taller than Fable, with broad, pointed ears.

"Is that . . . a goblin?" said Fable.

178

"Hello?" said Raina.

The creature shuffled to a halt, swaying slightly.

"Identify yourself," said Raina.

"Edge o' the fog," the creature mumbled lazily, as if talking in his sleep. "Got ta go back."

"Wait." Raina stepped closer. Her cloak sent the mists swirling in mesmerizing spirals that climbed up to her waist as she waded in. She stared at the little man, then shook her head as if trying to clear cobwebs from her mind. "Thief King?"

Fable strained her eyes to see the goblin's face. She had rarely seen the High Chief of the Hollowcliff Horde not wearing his signature top hat—the one with a plume of bright red cardinal feathers—but the figure before them did have the same nose, the same pale scar cutting through one eyebrow. "Chief Nudd?" she said. "Is that you?"

The goblin's eyes stared numbly forward, not showing any sign of recognition. "Got ta go back," he repeated. Then, with the shambling steps of a sleepwalker, Nudd turned and plodded away, back into the glowing clouds.

"Stop!" Raina plunged in after him, the mists swallowing her a little too eagerly. "Come back!"

"Wait for m—mm!" Fable began, but before she could finish, a hand slapped over her mouth and an arm grabbed her roughly from behind.

"MmmMMmph!" She tried to scream, but her voice was muffled. She could see her mother's shadow fading into the mist. She tried to spin away from her attacker, but the grip around her arms tightened and she was yanked backward. She bit down hard on the fingers covering her mouth and heard a sharp intake of breath from behind her—and then there were more hands, small and rough, clutching at her arms, her hair, her neck. Fable shuddered. Something was crawling all over her, snuffling and chittering. She kicked and wriggled, but before she could get her feet beneath her, she found herself yanked backward, and in an instant the whole world went all wrong.

The tunnel vanished with a dull *whoom*. The constant background noises of wind and droplets of water echoing in the distance abruptly silenced, and Fable's whole body felt oddly warm—like she had fallen backward into a hot spring, only this was definitely not water. Everything around her was dark and sticky, like she was swimming through molasses. She could feel herself moving, sliding through the darkness, but lifting her arm or raising a knee through the thick, warm fluid was harder than trying to push through the boggy mud of the mire.

Fable held her breath as long as she could, felt her lungs straining with effort. And then, as suddenly as it had begun, the sensation ended. Air rushed over her face, her ears began working again, and Fable fell to her knees in a new tunnel. Sparkling gems in the rocks lit the walls with a dim blue glow.

Fable gulped lungfuls of air for a few seconds and then spun to her feet in a graceful flurry of motion that might have looked impressive and intimidating . . . if she hadn't ended up with a face full of her own curly hair. She spat and batted it out of her eyes. Her knees bent, her fists balled, and she readied herself for a fight.

In front of her stood the woman in the austere gray dress. Her bristly pets nestled around her feet and on her shoulders.

"Madam Root," Fable growled. "What did you just do to me?"

"Nothing at all," said Madam Root. "My dear, sweet kobolds, on the other hand, have just taken you on a trip through solid stone. It's a neat little trick, isn't it? They've gotten quite good at it over the years. Hardly ever leave someone behind anymore. They live inside the rocks, don't you know? Cunning creatures."

"So you *are* the kidnapper after all," Fable snarled. "Well, you're not going to get away with it!"

Madam Root rolled her eyes. "I should have left you in twenty feet of bedrock. I already regret saving you."

"*Saving* me?" Fable snapped. "You didn't *save* me! You *stole* me!"

"Have you considered the possibility that I might have just done both?"

Fable hesitated. "Saved me from *what?*" She looked around. "Where did you take me? Where's my mama? Take me back to my mama *right now.*"

"Ugh. You stupid child. I tried to warn you both. But did you listen? No. You couldn't leave well enough alone, so you went deeper. And now your mother is gone."

"M-my mother's not gone. She went after Mr. Nudd. He's our friend, and friends don't just leave each other."

"*Everybody* leaves," said the woman, icily. "Eventually."

"Well, not *me!*" said Fable. "I'm getting my mama back right now! And Nudd, and Tinn, and Cole, and . . . and everybody!"

The woman regarded Fable.

"You want to know what's happened to your *mama?* What's probably happening to *all* of your friends right now?"

Fable's brow furrowed. Her fists were shaking.

"I'll show you." Madam Root spun on her heel without further discussion and strode away into the tunnel. The kobolds skittered along behind her, several of them diving into the stone floor and resurfacing a few feet farther along. They reminded Fable of otters as they swam.

She glanced around herself nervously. It was very empty. "Why should I trust you?" she yelled at the woman's back.

"You probably shouldn't," Madam Root replied without turning. "But you don't have a lot of other options at the moment, now, do you?"

Fable ground her teeth. Before the woman could vanish again, Fable jogged after her. "Okay. So where are you taking me?"

"They call it Delvers' Deep. Or they used to."

"Well," said Fable, when it became clear the woman was not going to explain further, "those are words, I guess. What's a delver?"

The woman walked briskly, so that Fable had to quickstep to keep up. "I remember when the delvers first came to my mountains, many centuries ago," she said. "They were such humble creatures, simple and earnest. They could commune with the bats, and my kobolds found them amusing."

"Can delvers do magic?"

"They could," she said, "once. They are related to elves—not that you would guess it to see them today, all hunched over and beady-eyed. The world changed, you see, a very long time ago. Magic moved on. The delvers did not. And so they became something else—something . . . less. Their skin grew more calloused with every passing generation, and their vision more narrow."

She slipped fluidly between a tight cleft in the rocks

183

and waited as Fable followed with considerably more scooting and scraping.

"They seemed to respect the earth, though," she continued when Fable was with her again, "and they shunned the daylight—so for a time I felt a kinship with them. I allowed them to carve out their space, shovelful by shovelful, within my domain. They believed in impossible dreams, and worshipped long-forgotten gods, and I found this charming, in a way. Their corner of the underground was a peaceful place, save for the rhythm of the picks and the axes. They were so determined, in those early days, so single-minded, and their toil amused me. They hated the world above with such blind zeal, and their hate amused me, too. It was not aimed at me, so what was the harm? I did not recognize it for what it was."

"What was it?"

"It was . . . the Beginning," said Madam Root gravely. The way she said it, Fable could practically hear the capital B. "I was on the foothills of a treacherous mountain that I was too shortsighted to see rising up in front of me. It was obvious what they were, even back then. They did not hide it. But I did let them carry on. They were so few, and their progress was so painstakingly slow—I did not fear their presence. I dare say I even *enjoyed* it at times—their quiet, diligent fury. What harm could such low creatures

184

cause?" The woman took a deep breath. "But the delvers who began the thing gave rise to the delvers who continued it. And those *new* delvers found *new* ways to hate. And all the while, they dug. Shovelful by shovelful. Generation after generation. Before I realized it, their humble burrow had become a great, domed cavern. Whenever I thought they might finally be satisfied, might finally let it rest, they found new depths to plumb. I never imagined they could actually achieve it, but this newest generation of delvers— they could be the ones to finally finish it."

"Finish *what?*" said Fable.

"You," said Madam Root. "*All* of you."

Fable's jaw tensed. "My mama won't let that happen."

Madam Root did not respond.

"What's it called now?" Fable said.

"Hm?" The woman in gray spared her a sideways glance over one shoulder.

"You said it *used* to be called Delvers' Deep. What do they call it *now?*"

"*They* call it the Low Temple," said the woman. "*I* call it the Cavern of Lost Souls." She drew to a stop finally, turning to face Fable properly. "Would you like to know why?"

The mouth of the tunnel opened into empty space. No stairway, no railing—there was simply a rocky path right up until there wasn't. And what *wasn't* was *massive*. Fable could barely see the far side. It was as if the whole world had flipped upside down, with a layer of clouds floating just below them like rolling red fields and a ceiling of stone that hung thousands of feet above them.

"Don't get too close to the fog," Madam Root cautioned. "Listen. Do you hear that?"

Fable listened. In the distance, she could make out the clink of metal on stone. It was coming from somewhere beneath the fog. "Is that delvers?"

Madam Root shook her head. "Not for many years now. The first delvers did their own digging. Diligent workers. These ones have long since found more insidious ways to make the rest of the world do their digging for them. It was only trespassers in the beginning—lost explorers and greedy miners who chiseled into their domain—nobody who would be missed. But when those captives proved useful, the delvers began capturing prisoners from above. They used to be cautious about it: one at a time, different species each time, never too many at once. They have grown more and more brazen of late."

Fable clenched her fists. "I want to see what's going on down there," she said.

"Go through that fog and you'll *be a part* of what's going on down there."

186

Fable drew a deep breath and said: "Gale."

It was nothing like the storm winds Fable could produce in the open air, but still Madam Root put out a hand to steady herself. The hem of her dress whipped in the breeze as a column of wind poured out of the tunnel behind them and cut down into the fog. It pushed the clouds aside just long enough for Fable to spy a crowd of at least a dozen figures far below, arranged along the bottom edge of the cavern. They hefted axes and hauled wheelbarrows, shuffling as they walked and swaying where they stood, all of them looking as mindless and exhausted as Chief Nudd. One worker appeared to have collapsed to the ground. He lay motionless as the others paid him no mind, stepping over the body as they went about their tasks. They were not one race. The smallest looked like gnats from this distance, and the largest looked like lumbering railway cars with fur. Fable picked out bushy-bearded gnomes, goat-legged satyrs, a scaly naga, and plenty more creatures she could not as easily identify before the mists melted back together into an inscrutable cloud bank.

"This is where they take the fortunate ones," Madam Root said. "The fog turns them into shadows first—makes them forget who they were. They cannot think for themselves or act against their new masters. They serve the order until they die for the order. If your mother is theirs now, she is not your mother anymore."

"No. Not my mama. They won't turn her. My mama is strong."

Madam Root sighed heavily. "More's the pity. The order likes the strong ones."

"She can turn into a bear! Maybe the mist doesn't work on animals!"

"Did you see the beasts down there? The big ones hauling away the loose rock?"

Fable nodded. Her chest felt heavy.

"Those are called kobbs. Distant relatives to the kobolds—an ancient race. Prehistoric kobbs carved these tunnels, even before my time. Impossibly powerful, graceful creatures. They can move mountains, yet they would not harm an earthworm. Do you know how many kobbs exist in the world today?"

Fable shook her head.

"Neither do I," said Madam Root. "Because they keep to themselves, sweet giants. There were seven in this region, until recently. The order has taken them all. Now they only work until they collapse. To the best of my knowledge, there are three still living."

"I get it!" Fable burst out. "I get it, okay? The delvers are the worst!"

"Not the *worst*." Madam Root shook her head. "The worst," she added soberly, "is what the delvers are waking up."

As if on cue, the earth shook. Dust and grit trickled down into Fable's hair.

Fable squared her jaw and stood as tall as she could. "I'm not running away from this."

Madam Root shrugged. "Just as well. Running would do you no good."

TWENTY

COLE RAN THROUGH THE TWISTING, SHADOWY corridors. He could hear the sounds of footsteps pounding after him, never farther away than a few bends in the serpentine tunnel.

They were catching up.

The floor pitched downward abruptly, and Cole lost his footing, tumbling uncontrollably down the slope. He pushed himself to his feet the moment he hit level ground again, but it was too late—heavy hands grabbed him by the shoulders and wrenched him aside.

"Get off of m—" he tried to shout, but a warm hand clapped over his mouth.

"Shh!" a voice shushed.

Cole's heart was hammering against his chest. He panted through his nose. His captor hauled him into a slim alcove in the rocks, no larger than a broom closet. There, the two of them stood, frozen, with Cole caught in a tight bear hug. Cole could feel the stranger's heavy breaths as they waited. He smelled like dirty laundry.

The sound of footsteps neared, and in a blur of light and flapping fabric, Tommy and the acolytes thundered past.

"The Low Priest is gonna feed your bones to the kobbs," one of them said.

"This is *not* my fault," Tommy's voice barked.

"Just find the brat," said another.

The footsteps faded gradually as the creatures raced off into the darkness.

The hand slowly lowered from Cole's mouth. "You do not want them to catch you," said the stranger. His voice was low and gravelly.

"Yeah. I picked up on that," Cole whispered.

The rough hands slowly released Cole, and the stranger peeked out of the alcove. In the darkness, Cole could not tell what sort of creature he was, but his hair was matted, his clothes were more dirt than fabric, and he smelled like musty leather.

"Come with me," the ragged figure whispered, then crept out into the tunnel the way they had come.

Cole glanced up and down the corridor nervously. It was never a good sign when your best option was running into the shadows with a dirty stranger—but he would have to take what he could get at this point. He followed as quietly as he could.

About twenty feet up the tunnel, the stranger planted one foot on the wall and pushed himself up to grab the lip of a wide crevice Cole hadn't even realized was there. He swung over the top and disappeared for a moment, then reached back down for Cole. "Come on. They don't come this way."

Cole took the proffered hand and looked into his rescuer's face for the first time. If the man hadn't had Cole's arm in a firm grip, Cole might have fallen over backward. That face. It was dirty, pale, and covered in a scruffy beard . . . but Cole knew that face like he knew his own.

The man hauled him up and through the crevice, depositing him on his feet in a new cave. This one was speckled with more of the shining blue stones, circling them like constellations in the night sky. He did not wait for Cole, but pressed onward, through another series of tunnels that twisted and turned until the passage opened into a wide chamber with a trickling waterfall on the far end. He plodded over to the waterfall and scooped out a drink for himself.

"Y-you're him." Cole's voice was barely a whisper.

The man turned, a puzzled look on his familiar face.

Cole stared at those cheekbones, his nose, those eyes. They were so like his own and like his brother's, and yet also different—a little wider here, a little sharper there. They were the features that had smiled out at Cole his entire life from the black-and-white photograph on the mantel. There was no mistaking that face. This man was Joseph Burton.

"Hello, young man," Joseph said. "You look so familiar. Have we met?"

Cole steeled himself. "I'm . . ." He swallowed, then raised his chin and looked his father in the eyes. "I'm Cole."

Joseph nodded. "Are you really? Good name. My wife and I had a good long talk about maybe calling our son Cole, actually. We'll have to make a final decision about that soon. It was going to be Thomas, but . . . it got complicated." He splashed his face and pushed his dirty hair back on his head. "Where are you from, Cole?"

Cole blinked. "Um. Endsborough."

"You live in Endsborough? I live in Endsborough, too!"

Cole hesitated. "I . . . I know. You're my . . . You . . ."
Cole took a steadying breath and tried to refocus. "Listen. I
had to grow up my whole life without a father."

"I'm so sorry to hear it, kid," Joseph interjected. "Looks
like you turned out all right, though, eh? There's a lot of
different paths up the mountain. I'm sure your mother
worked very hard."

"She works harder than you can imagine!" said Cole.
"She shouldn't *have* to work so hard. That's the whole
point. If you—"

"That's what I like to hear. Respect your mother, kid.
My Annie just became a mother. Still hard to believe we
have a son."

"You . . ." Cole floundered. "You have *two* sons."

"Nope, just the one. Well—it's complicated. I'm working on that. That's sort of why I came down here in the
first place."

Cole's mouth hung open.

Joseph didn't seem to notice. "Annie is a better mom
than I am a dad, that's for sure. But I'm picking it up as I
go. There are lots of exciting moments I'm looking forward
to. First steps. Hearing him say *Daddy* for the first time. I'll
figure out the fatherhood thing eventually." He began to
hum to himself, absently.

Cole stared at the man for a solid minute. "How long," he managed at last, "do you think you've been down here?"

"Oh!" Joseph started, as if surprised Cole was still there. "Hello, young man," he said genially. "You look so familiar. Have we met?"

TWENTY-ONE

Evie's hands shook as she raised them meekly above her head. "You caught me," she said.

The acolyte's crimson robes brushed the dusty ground. "Yes," he said. "Um. Yes, I did. I caught you. And now I'm going to take you to my leader."

Evie rolled her eyes. "You're not going to say it like that, are you?"

Tinn sighed. He swished his robes. "How about *you* play the part of the weird underground cult member and *I* can play myself as a kidnapping victim." He stretched his shoulders and swiveled his head this way and that on his neck. His changeling magic had worked smoothly, but

196

the acolyte's head still seemed too big for his body, and it made Tinn feel off-balance. "Are you sure this looks right? I didn't get a very long look."

"Shh." Evie put a finger over her lips. "I think someone's coming."

Voices carried down the zigzagging tunnel. "The Low Priest is gonna feed your bones to the kobbs," someone snarled in the distance.

"This is *not* my fault," barked another.

Tinn looked at Evie nervously through his overlarge eyes. Evie nodded resolutely.

"Just find the brat," said a third voice, nearer.

Tinn cleared his throat. "Get moving, you," he ordered, more loudly than was really necessary.

Footsteps rounded the corner, and in another moment three figures came hurrying into view. They all had the same squashed, bat-like faces. Two of them were acolytes, dressed in the same red robes as Tinn—the third was clad in workman's clothes. On his head sat a miner's helmet.

"Hey, look," said one of the red robes. "Korvum's caught the little rat. Good work, Korvum."

"Erm, yeah," mumbled Tinn. "I just caught this, erm, nasty child hiding in the caves." He felt sweat run down his new, leathery skin. He was not getting the accent right, he just knew it. The acolyte he was copying had sounded slightly more nasal, hadn't he? Did he have a hint of a lisp also? Ugh. Changing was hard.

The man in the mining helmet scowled and looked Evie up and down. "That's not the same kid," he said.

"No?" the first red robe grunted. "How can you tell? Uplanders all start to look the same after a while."

The one in the miner's helmet threw up his hands. "He was a *boy*, you clod. This one's *female*. I *told* you there were more of them snooping around."

"Watch the tone," spat the first robe. "I'm not the one who let the boy run off."

Tinn's heart thudded. They had to be talking about Cole. And they hadn't caught him yet. That was good.

"Well?" The one in the helmet turned back to Tinn. "You taking this one for conversion or what?"

"Uh. Yeah." Tinn nodded his heavy head. "Conversion."

"I thought you said you were going to take me to the *Low Altar*," Evie said meaningfully.

"Right," said Tinn. "That's right, you dirty human. Low Altar first, obviously. To watch the hob, erm, the sacrifice. Then I'm taking her right over to conversion after that."

"Serpent's teeth, that's right," the red robe said. "Forgot you got yourself on the shortlist for Low Order. The priest will be starting any minute now. You should already be there."

"Yup," Tinn said. "So I'll just be going, then."

"You can leave her with us," said the other acolyte. "We'll run her through the mist with the other one, once we track him down."

Evie's eyes widened.

"No," said Tinn abruptly. "No, um, I'm the one who found her. So, I should be the one to, erm, convert her. I'll do it. I'm fine. Thank you."

"You sure you can keep her under control?" said the helmeted one. "Human children can be surprisingly scrappy."

"I'm very small and weak," said Evie, adding a raspy cough. "And sickly."

The red robe leaned his face close to Tinn, his beady eyes narrowing. "Don't want to share credit? Trying to curry favor from the Low Priest before the final offering?"

Tinn felt a bead of sweat run down his neck. "Pretty much," he managed.

The red robe nodded. "Respect that. Fair enough. All right. Let's go find that runner."

The two red robes and the one in the miner's helmet plodded off down the tunnel while Tinn and Evie stood in shocked silence for several seconds.

"That should never have worked," whispered Evie.

"I think I was very convincing," said Tinn. "So, are we still doing this?"

"My uncle Jim has a saying about nasty chores and other stuff you don't wanna do," said Evie. "*Sometimes the only way to get out of it is just to go through with it.*"

"Somehow I don't think your uncle Jim was thinking about walking into the middle of a murderous cult's secret ceremony when he said that."

"Mostly it was about horse poop," Evie admitted.

"Well, we're in the thick of the poop now. Let's go through with it."

Evie nodded. She took a deep breath, and then the two of them plunged into the shadowy passageway.

The deeper they went, the hotter and muggier the air in the tunnel felt. The corridor wound back and forth a dozen more times before it opened up into a truly enormous cavern. Thick clouds hung fifty feet above them, churning and swirling, making it impossible to see the ceiling of the massive cave. Halfway across the yawning cavern, a broad stone column rose from the ground until it disappeared into the clouds.

The ground under their feet was black and lumpy, like the bottom of a pan left to ruin on a hot stove. It steamed from tiny fissures that spider-webbed across the surface. Where the cracks were widest, Tinn could see ripples of heat and a red glow that emanated from somewhere beneath the crust.

"Is that lava?" Tinn whispered from out of the corner of his wide mouth.

"Magma," whispered Evie. "When it's underground it's called magma."

"We can't possibly be far enough down for that to be real, actual magma, can we? We would have to be miles beneath the surface."

"I have no idea," whispered Evie. "I'm a little more interested in the creepy cult guys."

Hundreds of crimson-clad acolytes were amassing near the base of the central pillar. The whole congregation seemed to be glowing as the light from below met their robes in ripples of bloodred fabric.

Somewhere within the group, the frightened hob was crying. Evie took a deep breath. "Let's get closer."

Tinn pressed forward, one hand gripping Evie's shoulder tightly.

They made their way to the edge of the crowd. Hundreds of robed figures all had their eyes turned toward the base of the central pillar, where a broad half-moon had been cut into the blackened earth. It was at least twenty feet across at its widest points, and it opened into a pool of roiling liquid rock. Tinn could feel the heat pouring out of it. It was hotter even than the heat he had felt back when the Fenerty's Paper Goods building had burned down. The way the surface of the glowing pool churned and bubbled, Tinn could almost imagine something just below the crust, weaving and twisting like an eel wriggling in cloudy waters. The patterns changed constantly, darkening in patches to a burnt brown and flaring up now and then to an almost blinding yellow. Gazing into the pit was like trying to stare at the sun through shifting clouds, and in the end Tinn had to look away. A crescent-shaped altar of black stone overlooked the magma pool, and it was onto this platform that the Low Priest was now rising. Two acolytes rose behind him, the simpering hob held between them. The Thing came gliding up the steps last, hovering to a stop beside the priest. Where its shadows met the light of the pit, the air rippled and warped.

A hush fell over the assembly as the Low Priest took his position, and the only sounds that remained were the gurgling crackle of the pit and the sniffling cries of the hob.

"Loyal acolytes," the Low Priest called out ceremoniously, "it is time."

TWENTY-TWO

"HELLO, YOUNG MAN," SAID JOSEPH. "YOU LOOK so familiar. Have we met?"

Cole took a deep breath. "Yeah. We've done this part. A few times now. Can you remember anything at all?"

"Of course. I remember the important things," said Joseph. "I have a son, did you know?"

"Two sons," said Cole.

"Mm." Joseph scowled. "Not exactly. The other is—"

"My brother," said Cole.

"Brother?" Joseph blinked and focused on Cole with some effort.

"Yeah," Cole said. "I have a twin brother."

"That must be nice. Is he just like you?"

"Mostly." Cole sighed. "He worries more."

"Don't you worry?"

"I don't know. I guess. I try not to."

Joseph nodded. "Nothing wrong with worrying. I worry all the time."

Cole caught himself watching the man's eyes. Beneath the beard and the matted hair, those eyes looked a lot like Tinn's.

"Heck. I don't think I'm ever *not* worrying," Joseph went on. "I have a son, did you know?"

Cole sighed. "Two sons," he repeated.

"Mm? Right, yes—there is a second one now. A change-ling. Wicked thing, or so I'm told. Twice as much to worry about there. I don't like leaving Annie alone with them, but she insisted—and I can't afford to stay home." Joseph's fingers fidgeted unconsciously with the cuff of his jacket.

"He's not wicked," said Cole. "He's good. You should know that."

"Mm." Joseph nodded, but his brow was creased and his gaze had drifted off down the empty tunnel.

"Do you understand me? I know you were scared and probably super confused about the second baby showing up, but Tinn turned out to be pretty great, actually."

"Mm? Good. That's good."

"So . . . you can stop worrying about the whole change-ling thing," said Cole.

Joseph glanced back at him. "Oh, I was worrying well before the changeling arrived."

Now it was Cole whose brow wrinkled. "What else are you worried about?"

Joseph shrugged. "What was I *not* worried about? I was worried I wouldn't know what to do when my baby cried. I was worried he'd get sick and I wouldn't know how to make him better. I was worried we wouldn't have enough money to get him nice things. That's why I took on all the extra shifts. But now that I'm working so much, I'm beginning to worry that . . . that I won't . . ."

"What?" said Cole.

"I'm worried I won't be there," said Joseph. "I'm worried my kid is gonna grow up not really knowing his dad."

Cole's throat felt tight.

"I don't want that." Joseph's voice was heavy and tired. "I don't want to not be there for my son. I don't want him to not know how much I love him."

Cole's eyes stung. "Then why—?" His voice failed him and he cleared his throat to try again. The words that emerged came out weak and brittle. "Then why didn't you come *home?*"

Joseph tilted his head, his gaze falling in and out of

focus on Cole's face. For a fraction of a second their eyes met, and a wave of painful recognition flicked across the man's face. He shook his head and closed his eyes, swallowing hard. After a moment his head sagged and his shoulders slumped.

"Dad?" Cole tried.

Joseph lifted his chin slowly. Cole could see his eyes were glistening and rimmed with red. "Hello, young man," he said. "You look so familiar. Have we met?"

Cole stared at his father.

Joseph gave Cole the sort of smile a substitute teacher gives a student they've never seen before.

"I can't take this," said Cole. "We need to get everyone out of these stupid tunnels and get home."

"Not just yet," said Joseph. "There's something I need to do first."

"What could possibly be more important than going home with your family?"

"Saving them," said Joseph.

"Ugh. They don't *need* saving—the changeling *isn't* wicked. We've already done this bit."

"Not saving them from the changeling," Joseph said.

Cole's brow creased. "Then saving them from *what*, exactly?"

"From the end of the world, of course."

TWENTY-THREE

FABLE HELD HER BREATH AS SHE DRIFTED DOWN into the rocky floor, a kobold perched on either shoulder. According to Madam Root, who had melted into the earth first, it *was* possible to breathe the stones just as the kobolds did—but it was important to exhale all of them before emerging, because the rocks were still rocks whether you could breathe them or not.

It was impossible for Fable to judge how far they had traveled by the time they emerged, feetfirst, out of the ceiling of another chamber. If Madam Root had been telling the truth, they were now somewhere beneath the cloud layer in the heart of the Low Order's territory.

Fable looked around. They were not in the huge cavern they had seen from above, but in a much smaller chamber about as big as the Burtons' front room. The walls here did not have the knobby, natural texture of the tunnels. They were carved and sanded smooth and were etched with pictures. The same glowing blue gems that had naturally speckled the corridor above had been carefully planted within the lines of each etching, so that the light in the room came from the pictures themselves.

"This is a sacred chamber," said Madam Root. "Only the lowest of the low priests are allowed in here. They've nearly caught me once or twice, but they will all be at their awful ceremony right now."

"You've snuck in here before?" said Fable. "Why?"

"Because I wish to understand what drives them. These carvings were made generations ago. Can you read what they say?" She gestured at the first glowing illustration. It depicted a big snake coiled within a circle, and beneath it were letters that did not look like any language Fable had ever seen.

Fable shook her head.

"It says: *In fire, beneath the Delvers' Deep, long does the coiled serpent sleep.* More or less. It sounds more formal in Ancient Delver. The Low Order worships the fire serpent. It is a primal, elemental creature. Very old magic."

Fable nodded and followed Madam Root farther down the wall.

"Let's see, here it says that the serpent sings to them. This bit is about the first priest summoned to dig here."

"I recognize this one!" Fable pointed to an image a little way down. "A prophet gave this symbol to my friend. It's why we're down here. What does it mean?"

"*The temple walls and hallowed halls must be complete before the fall,*" said Madam Root. "This is their entire way of life. Their kind have been preparing this temple for generations. There was always the promise that completing it would bring about the end, but I had allowed myself to imagine that it was all a metaphor—that there would never be a fall."

"What's *the fall?*"

"When the earth collapses into itself and the serpent awakens to cleanse the world with its fires."

"Wait—what? The *whole* world?"

"Pretty standard apocalypse, really."

"Why would anybody *want* that?"

Madam Root shrugged. "Perhaps because hating everybody else can be easier than taking care of yourself." She skipped over a few more pictures and stopped in front of an image Fable didn't understand. "This depicts the first portent of destruction. It is an omen that the delvers' apocalypse is finally at hand. The delvers carved it centuries ago. It came true this year."

"What is it supposed to be?"

"Don't look at the lights," said Madam Root. "Look at the dark spot in the center."

Fable tilted her head and suddenly found herself looking at something like a big wolf made from the empty bit where the lights weren't.

"*With night's descent and shadows bent, beware the darkling's discontent,*" read Madam Root.

"The Thing," whispered Fable.

"*The Thing?*" said Madam Root. "You've encountered the darkling before?"

"I guess. Sort of. It snuck into my forest a while back and set up a nest of creepy black brambles," Fable explained. "But we fought against it last summer and scared it away after it tried to eat one of my friends."

"So *you* sent the darkling underground?" Madam Root raised an eyebrow. "You're the ones who delivered the delvers their first portent."

Fable held up her hands. "We just kicked its butt. We didn't know it was gonna start an apocalypse!"

Madam Root took a deep breath. "It is only the first portent," she said. She pointed farther down the wall. "They also believe there will be a mighty war between the human world and the magic world, during which giants will rise up against one another."

Fable winced. "Yeah. We sort of did that already, too. What else is going to happen?"

Madam Root looked at Fable and then back to the wall. "The last portent is about a *prince*. Being the daughter of a queen, you wouldn't happen to know any *princes*, would you? Because once they've offered the prince to their Ancient One, then the whole thing comes crashing down, everybody dies, and the snake burns up the world."

Fable considered. "Nope. No princes. I've met a gnome king, and I know a dog called Duke. What's the prophecy say, exactly?"

"The prince of lies and mirror guise will take his place as sacrifice."

"Mirror guys?" said Fable.

"Mirror guise," repeated Madam Root. "It's describing a shapeshifter who takes the appearance of others."

"Oh." A cold weight dropped into Fable's stomach. "Oh. Yeah. I do know somebody who can do that."

TWENTY-FOUR

Tɪɴɴ ᴅɪᴅɴ'ᴛ ᴋɴᴏᴡ ʜᴏᴡ ᴍᴜᴄʜ ʟᴏɴɢᴇʀ ʜᴇ could keep up his transformation. He kept one hand on Evie's shoulder and took deep breaths as the Low Priest began to speak.

"Ancient One, we humbly make our daily sacrifice."

"Psst. Korvum?" a voice whispered.

Tinn glanced to his right, where a tall, lanky acolyte was standing. She had a slightly longer face than the one Tinn wore, and her squashed-up nose was more like a pig's than a bat's. Tinn swallowed and smiled as casually as he could manage at the hooded figure, then stopped smiling because that felt like the wrong response.

"You know you're not supposed to bring uplanders to the sacrifices," the acolyte hissed, her eyes flicking to the altar and back at Evie, who scooted a little farther away from her.

"Who, her?" said Tinn. "She's a . . . a spare. In case that hob up there isn't enough for the Ancient One. You know how it is when you have a little snack and it just makes you hungrier? Don't want the Ancient One to go hungry."

The acolyte narrowed her eyes. "The Ancient One is *ever hungry*," she said, as if this were an obvious fact. "It is the sacred serpent's destiny to devour the *whole of the earth*."

Tinn swallowed. "Right."

"I'm more filling than I look," offered Evie.

The acolyte looked aghast. "It talks?" She backed up a step. "It still needs to be converted!"

Nearby acolytes turned at the sound of her voice.

"I'm on top of it," insisted Tinn in an urgent whisper. "All under control."

"Who dares speak during tribute?" the Low Priest's voice suddenly boomed over the crowd.

The assembly parted until a corridor straight to the altar opened in front of Evie and Tinn.

"I—I dare," said Evie.

Tinn's head was reeling. "What are you doing?" he breathed, gripping her shoulder even tighter, but Evie went on.

"If you're so afraid of this Ancient One," Evie called up to the priest, "then why do you keep *feeding* it?"

"Afraid?" The Low Priest laughed bitterly. "Child, what under earth made you think we were afraid?"

"I don't know. Maybe the fact that you're hiding in a hole in the ground and throwing people into lava because you think some monster is going to devour the earth if you don't."

The priest smiled a wide, joyless smile. "Our sacrifices do not *prevent* the Ancient One from rising, simple creature," he said. "They *encourage* it."

The magma behind him gurgled and spat.

"*Your* sacrifices?" Evie went on. "Seems like you let everyone else do the sacrificing except for you."

"I-I'm sorry, um, Low Priest," Tinn managed, trying to keep his face concealed behind the hood. "I will remove the human."

"No." The priest was unruffled. "Let this be a moment of enlightenment. Remember well, believers—we were chosen for this destiny. It is our sacred role to awaken the Ancient One, as it is the role of the unworthy to melt into the ashes. This holy task was not ours to begin, but by the grace of the great serpent of fire, it will be ours to see it done. Our ancestors heard the serpent's song when no one else could. It called to them, just as it calls to us—let it

214

awaken in each of you the truth of our sacred mission."
A low, tuneless hum started somewhere within the crowd
and was echoed by a dozen more voices, droning out the
same solemn notes. The priest nodded. "We will rouse the
slumbering god who dwells at the center of the world so
that the serpent's divine fires might cleanse the unworthy
from the earth at last. It is foretold."

"*That's* what this is all about?" Tinn said.

"Just to be clear," Evie said, "some big snake sang your
grandparents a song, and that's the reason you're murdering
people and hoping to kill the whole world?" She glanced
at the hooded faces all around her. "And that feels reason-
able and normal to you all? Even when you hear it out
loud?"

The humming quieted.

"Your feeble mind could not comprehend our higher
purpose," the Low Priest answered. "Enough of this. I have
entertained an interruption for too long." He waved a hand
at the Thing, which rippled to attention. "Darkling, kill
the girl."

"No!" Tinn yelled. His hood fell back, but he did his
best to maintain the acolyte disguise. His heart was racing.

The Low Priest stared at him for several long seconds
before he spoke. "That face," the priest said at last, his voice
a guttural purr, "is not yours."

"Oh, this?" Tinn's throat felt tight. Things were going about as disastrously as he should have expected. "Well, that guy you killed wasn't using it anymore, so . . ."

The Low Priest did not yell or grimace or startle. Instead, his wide lips bent slowly into an unsettling smile. Hushed whispers crept through the assembly. *"The prince of lies,"* Tinn could hear over the murmurs.

Every eye was now on Tinn, with those farthest away craning their necks over robed shoulders to catch a glimpse. The Low Priest stepped down from the podium, taking slow, steady paces, his gaze locked on Tinn.

"Look, I didn't mean to interrupt your get-together," Tinn managed. "I just wanted to find my friends and get out of your hair. So . . . everyone can just stay calm. There's no need to be mad."

"Mad? You have not made me mad, little mimic." The Low Priest came to a halt directly in front of Tinn. "On the contrary, you have made me happier than you will ever know. Your presence is a *gift.* A gift I intend to see properly *given.*" And with that, he grabbed Tinn by the front of his robes.

Evie grabbed for the priest's arms, but hands emerged from the crowd to restrain her. "Let go!" she yelled.

Tinn kicked and struggled as the priest dragged him up the stony steps of the altar. He could feel panic setting in and his magic failing him at last. The robes shifted and shrank as his feet dragged across the dusty stones—until soon the priest was holding a bruised, scruffy-haired boy by his dirty shirtfront.

Atop the altar, with Tinn still struggling in his grip, the Low Priest once more addressed the crowd. "Momentous news, believers. This ceremony has just been elevated. *The prince of lies and mirror guise,*" he boomed, "*will take his place as sacrifice.*"

"What exactly do you mean, *the end of the world?*" said Cole.

"It's fuzzy." Joseph put his hands to his temples. He looked like he was fighting back a nasty headache.

"Try," pleaded Cole. "Let's go back. What's the first thing you can remember after leaving work?"

"I remember . . . falling," said Joseph. "I fell a long way down. I remember a stranger with a lamp, and then . . . I remember waking up. I think some time might have passed. Maybe even a few days?"

"Maybe a little bit more than a few days," said Cole, gravely.

"I was still underground when I woke up," Joseph continued. "And there were these men—or things—all dressed in red. They were walking me toward something—toward the fog, I think." Joseph grabbed Cole's arm. "Stay away from the fog!"

"What happened next?" Cole asked. "The men in red?"

"Everything got dark. There was something with us in the tunnel. A shadow. It was icy cold, and I was confused, so I ran. I ran and hid. The men in red were frightened. I know it sounds mad, but I think the shadow . . . attacked them, if you can imagine it."

"Yeah. I can imagine it."

"But then I heard them. More hooded people arrived, filling the tunnel, but they didn't fight the shadow. They spoke to it. They told it that if it worked with them, then they would give it more lives to eat, more misery and pain. They promised they would deliver to it *the end of the world.* That's what they said. *The end of the world.* I was having trouble keeping my thoughts straight, but I told myself to remember that part. I said it to myself over and over so I wouldn't forget."

"That's a pretty good detail to hang on to," said Cole.

"Thanks," said Joseph. "Hang on a moment. You . . . you look so familiar. Have we met?"

"Stay with me," urged Cole. "Did the red robes say anything about how the world was going to end?"

Joseph looked pained. "Something about the central pillar?" he said.

Cole's face fell. "Yeah, that would do it." He pulled the disc out of his pocket and looked at the design again. "Everything rests on the central pillar. If they break that, then the whole thing collapses. The Wild Wood. Endsborough. All of it goes down."

Joseph nodded. "I can't let that happen. There are people in Endsborough I need to protect. I have a son."

"I know," sighed Cole. "You have two." Cole paused. His father's brow was already creased with the strain of holding so many thoughts in his head. "Your family isn't *in* Endsborough right now. They're down *here*. I don't know where Tinn is, but those bad guys in the red hoods, they took Mom. They have Annie."

"My Annie?" Joseph's eyes widened. "They stole her?"

"They stole you, too. Can you remember where they took you?"

Joseph's brow wrinkled with concentration. "I . . . I don't remember. I was only under their control for a few hours, I think . . ."

"It was more than a few hours."

". . . Days?"

"A *lot* of days. Please, try to remember. Where did they keep you?"

Joseph took a deep breath. "There might have been a sort of a barracks, I think. It opened up onto the big chamber with the pillar in the middle." He rubbed the bridge of his nose. "Yes. I think I can remember it."

"Great. How do we get back to the big chamber?"

Joseph scowled. "How many days?"

"What?"

"How many days have I been lost?"

Cole read the confusion and frustration in his father's eyes and it made his chest hurt. His dad looked like he was trying to read an important letter, but the ink was all smudged. Cole took a deep breath. "Give me your hands."

Warily, Joseph held out his hands.

Cole lifted the rough, calloused palms to his cheeks until Joseph was cupping his son's face in his fingers for the first time in thirteen years. "About this many," said Cole.

He let go of his father's hands, but Joseph did not drop his arms right away. He stayed there, staring into Cole's eyes like he might get lost in them. "I know you," he managed.

"We need to find where they're keeping the prisoners," said Cole, pulling away. His throat felt tight.

"Right," said Joseph. "Stay with me. And whatever you do, do not let the Low Priest get his hands on you."

Tinn had given up struggling. The Low Priest's grip hadn't budged, and even if Tinn had broken it, there was a crowd of a hundred acolytes behind him and a pit of liquid magma ahead. His options were less than great. He could feel the searing heat billowing up from the magma pool while the Low Priest shoved him into position on the altar. It made his vision swim.

The Low Priest, still holding Tinn firmly by the lapels, began to hum. It was a deep, rumbling sound, not like a proper song, but more like a force of nature. It rose and fell the way trees groan before they topple or the way thunder grumbles during a storm. Around him, a hundred red-robed acolytes hummed along in unison.

"If you're going to kill me, do you really need to make it so creepy?" Tinn managed.

The heat suddenly abated, and a cool breeze swept over him. Tinn peeked out of one eye. Ribbons of oily black shadows rippled in the air in front of him, rising to take an almost human shape.

NO, said the Thing.

The Low Priest narrowed his eyes at the inky figure.

"Back away, darkling," the Low Priest growled. "Your wait is nearly over. You will feast on a bounty of torture and torment the likes of which this world has never known. I am about to give the world to the Ancient One, and then you can gorge yourself on the misery that follows."

NO, repeated the Thing. NOT THAT ONE.

221

The Low Priest scowled. "You dare to—"

But the Low Priest didn't finish. Tattered ribbons of shadow caught him by the throat and whipped around his arms and legs. Tinn staggered back, away from them both.

Hooded acolytes swept toward the altar in defense of the priest, but the Thing was faster. Jagged spears like fluid obsidian shot out and back, piercing through one red robe after another, and writhing vines of darkness coiled around those who remained standing.

"Why?" croaked the priest.

I DO NOT KNOW, answered the Thing, flatly.

"You could have had . . . such exquisite miseries," the Low Priest wheezed.

I WILL CONTENT MYSELF WITH YOURS. The Thing's shadows trembled around the priest's neck.

The priest smiled back at it.

I HAVE THWARTED YOUR SACRED PLANS. I HAVE KILLED YOUR MOST DEVOTED FOLLOWERS. YOUR DEATH IS A CERTAINTY. YET YOU DO NOT DESPAIR, said the Thing. WHY?

"You have not thwarted anything," the priest rasped. "It was always going to end this way. It has all been leading to this, the song that has echoed in our skulls for generations. And now . . ." His eyes glistened with the golden-orange glow of the magma. ". . . *Finish it!*"

The Thing gave a rippling shrug. VERY WELL.

In a flurry, all of the ribbons of shadow receded back into the Thing, sending the Low Priest spinning backward over the end of the altar.

Tinn stared. He could not look away as the mad priest cackled, tumbling through the air, arms spread wide. He could not look away as the priest's body struck the boiling surface and those brilliant robes caught fire. He could not look away as the glowing magma slowly began to envelop what was left.

"Why did you do it?" Tinn managed at last.

IT IS PECULIAR. The Thing's shadows wavered like smoke in a gentle breeze. I SAW THAT YOUR SUFFERING WAS IMMINENT, BUT I DID NOT WISH IT. SO I PREVENTED IT. THAT FELT . . . RIGHT. THAT SENSATION IS STRANGE TO ME. I DO NOT DISLIKE IT.

Tinn glanced down at the ashy remains in the magma pool one more time. The sigil that had hung around the Low Priest's neck was still just visible in the center of the charred pile.

"Well, I definitely would have disliked experiencing *that*." Tinn looked back at the Thing. "So . . . thank you?"

I ENJOYED MAKING OTHERS SUFFER AND DIE ON YOUR BEHALF. I WOULD DO IT AGAIN.

"That really doesn't need to become a regular thing."

Like creeping molasses, the magma finally pulled the last of the Low Priest down beneath its glowing surface, and with a faint *snap*, barely audible over the steady crackling, the sigil shattered.

And with the tiny *snap* of that pendant, the apocalypse clicked into motion.

TWENTY-FIVE

EVIE STARED UP AT THE THING STANDING BESIDE Tinn on the altar. The cavern was spinning around her. It had all happened in a blur. She had heard the stories, but witnessing the creature of darkness in action was more terrifying than she had imagined. All around her, red-robed corpses lay where they had fallen.

Evie was no coward. She had once run through the middle of a raging battle between humans and magical creatures to save her uncle—but in the end, everyone had miraculously survived that fight. This had been the opposite. There had been no battle in which to be brave, just a ruthless whirlwind of shadows. And now Evie was wading in a sea of death, feeling it wash up against her with every heartbeat. She felt empty and weightless and impossibly heavy all at the same time.

She stared up at the Thing. Out of habit, the one part of her brain that wasn't going quietly numb began trying to conceive of how she could capture the smoky, fluid patchwork of shadows on paper for her journal. How did you draw something like that? The constant rippling movement. The icy chill. The raw brutality.

Snap.

Evie blinked. She glanced down at her feet. Had the acolyte in front of her just moved? She nudged the body with her foot. A shard of broken stone slipped from the folds of the robes, and she flinched as it hit the ground with a faint *click*.

Crack. Snap. Clink.

She looked left and right. All around her, she could see little lights, like glowing embers, flickering to life atop the fallen bodies. She shook her head. What was happening?

An acolyte beside her had perished on his back, and she glanced down at him just in time to watch the sigil hanging from his chest glow red-hot and then burst to pieces with a *snap*.

Click. Crack. Snap. All of them were wearing the sign. And all of the signs were shattering.

"Tinn," she managed to call out with a voice that sounded small even in her own ears. "I think something's happening."

"We're almost there," Joseph whispered.

Cole nodded. The main chamber was just around the bend; he would have been able to sense it even if his father had not said anything. The air, for one, was warmer as they neared the cavern of Delvers' Deep.

More than the air, Cole's right leg was starting to feel warm, too. Hot, even. Painful. What the heck? He reached into his pocket and pulled out the disc. "Ow! Ow! Ow!" He dropped it on the path. The little symbol was glowing red-hot as it clattered onto the rocks.

"What's it doing?" asked Joseph.

"I don't know. It's never done that before."

With a *crack*, the stone suddenly shattered into half a dozen uneven pieces. The light gradually faded and the shards lay still and quiet on the tunnel floor.

"Somehow, I feel like that was a bad omen," Cole moaned.

Fable emerged from the solid stone wall of Delvers' Deep with a gasp. The kobold around her shoulders chittered unhappily and buried itself behind her curls. The air down here was muggier then it had been in the tunnels, and the sheer size of the cave in front of her made her head spin. Or, possibly, she had to consider that the feeling had more to do with the hazy layer of mind-addling clouds hovering far too close for comfort in the air above their heads.

"Something's wrong," said Madam Root, sliding free of the wall beside her.

"You mean other than a kidnapping snake cult trying to kill my friend and destroy the world?"

"Yes, obviously other than that," Madam Root hissed. "There's something in the air. I can feel it."

"Hm." Fable knew how to feel the air. Her mother had been training her to do it for most of her life. She closed her eyes and reached out with her other senses. "Wait. You're right," she said. "This place has some heavy magic in it. Oof. Bad magic."

"Oh! What have they done to you?"

Fable opened her eyes. Madam Root was hurrying along the floor of the cavern toward one of the cult's burly work animals—kobbs, she had called them. She had said they were a relative of the kobolds, but the huge beast looked more like a broad-mouthed guinea pig, if a guinea pig could grow to be the size of a locomotive. The colossal creature was standing near the cavern wall, all alone, swaying ever so slightly. Its eyes, wider than dinner plates, were glassy and unresponsive. Fable hurried to catch up with Madam Root.

"Do you remember me, old friend?" Madam Root was saying.

The kobb just stared off into the distance.

"Oh, they branded you! You! A spirit of these mountains! Like you were some common upland steer!" Fable followed Madam Root's furious eyes to the creature's chest. The coarse hairs had, indeed, been shaved back, and the treelike design of the Low Order had been seared into the poor thing's hide. "We are going to set you free. I swear it."

"I'm all for doing that," said Fable. "But what about my friends? My mama? We need to find her."

"If they've been taken captive, there are only so many places they could be. You've already seen the work crews." She gestured toward the walls in the far distance, where Fable could barely make out the hazy shapes of a dozen figures milling about. "Anytime they're not on the crews, they shuffle mindlessly back to the prisoner cabins." Madam Root pointed to a tunnel in the wall to the left. "Every once in a while the Low Order makes them walk back through the mists just to keep them good and mesmerized, but other than that"—she hesitated, her eyes narrowing as she peered toward the central pillar—"the only other place they might go would be to the altar for sacrifice."

Fable followed Madam Root's gaze. Far away, lit from behind by the warm orange of the magma pool, people were standing at the altar.

The eerie silence of the cavern was suddenly split by a deafening bellow. Fable threw her hands over her ears and spun around. The kobb was shaking, tossing its enormous head back and forth. Madam Root held up her arms to calm the beast, but it knocked her aside like she was nothing. The sigil branded into the kobb's chest was glowing red-hot. Fable leapt out of the way as the creature lurched forward. It belted out another roar, and then its gargantuan muscles flexed and it vaulted into the air. It bounded in a wide arc over Fable and Madam Root before diving down into the stony floor like it was water. The ground shuddered as the kobb moved through the charred rocks like an enormous koi skimming through a muddy pond. In its wake, the rocks rippled for only a moment before they regained their solidity.

Fable gasped. "It's going for the central pillar!"

"Then we're too late," breathed Madam Root.

Fable clenched her fists. "No such thing."

Tinn tore his eyes away from the magma pool as a roar echoed through the underground chamber. Something was hurtling toward them from the far side of the cavern. It swam through the stone floor like a shark cutting through ocean currents, surfacing and diving as it neared. The enormous shape was closing on them by the second.

"What *is* that?" he managed.

And then his vision went black as a wave of icy darkness swept around him. He felt the lurch of movement and tried to reach out his arms to steady himself, but they were pinned to his sides as if he had been rolled up in a thick, wet blanket. He knew the Thing's grasp only too well—his bones ached with its unnatural cold. But then, as quickly as it had overtaken him, the darkness ebbed away. It dripped off of him like oil at first, and then vanished like smoke in a breeze, and the searing heat of the cavern returned in a rush. Tinn wobbled unsteadily on his feet for a moment. Evie was a dozen paces ahead of him. He had been pulled fifty feet back from the altar and now stood facing it and the towering column behind it. The Thing took shape beside him.

"Did you just—" he began.

And then the altar exploded as the bristling kobb breached the surface one final time.

The beast sailed high over the magma pool—demonstrating astonishing grace for a rodent the size of a house—and slid directly into the central pillar with a sound like a great boulder splashing into a placid lake.

The cavern was deathly silent for five of the longest seconds Tinn had ever experienced, and then the kobb burst out the other side of the stone column. It slammed to the ground and kept going, bounding off toward the other end of the cavern and into the safety of the rocks beyond.

A noise was coming from the central pillar, a muffled crunching, like when someone tries to eat crackers in the back of the classroom during reading time without anybody noticing. *Crunch.* A sharp crack appeared on the surface of the column. *Crunch, crunch.* The crack expanded, stretched, and was joined by a spiderweb of smaller fractures.

"Run!" yelled Evie, and Tinn did not need to be told twice.

Behind them, the central pillar—the single column on which the enormous cavern, the town of Endsborough, and the whole of the Wild Wood were balanced—cracked in half.

TWENTY-SIX

THE GROUND SHUDDERED BENEATH FABLE'S feet as she pelted across the charred terrain. Just a hundred feet to her right, a hailstorm of rocks as wide as carriage wheels blasted the ground into jagged craters. Twenty feet to her left, a cleft in the floor abruptly widened with a groan, accompanied by a hiss of heat and a burst of ruby light. Her eyes watered, but she could see the central pillar ahead of her, the fractures spreading through it and the whole column shaking. It wouldn't hold for much longer.

She heard the slap of running feet and spotted a familiar pair of faces rushing toward her.

"Fable!" cried Evie.

Fable's eyes flicked from Evie to Tinn, and then back to the pillar. "You two get out of here!" she yelled to her friends. "Find cover if you can!" She spared them a momentary hopeful smile, then pressed forward with a determined burst of speed.

"Fable!" Tinn yelled after her. "What are you *doing*?"

"I don't know yet!" Fable called back. "But I intend to do it *swiftly* and *decisively*!"

The whole cavern shook again, and one of the horizontal supports that hung high above them splintered into a dozen pieces and fell, spinning, downward. The shards slammed to earth on all sides of Fable, striking like tree-sized javelins as she ran. Several of them hit with enough force to punch holes straight through the ground and into the hellish magma below. Heat billowed up through the freshly pierced vents.

Fable tried frantically to think while the world fell apart around her. She needed to reinforce the pillar, and fast. This deep beneath the surface, there were no roots to summon—and even if there were, her usual net of woven vines wouldn't be enough to hold up an entire forest. The remains of the altar platform were crumbling, stone by stone, tumbling into the pit below with bursts of light as the magma splashed and swallowed them. The heat was like a wall, and Fable could get no closer to the pillar without somehow crossing the rapidly widening pool of magma.

The pillar let out a deep croak. With horror, Fable saw that the whole top of the column had shifted several inches away from the bottom, sliding along the largest crack. She had to do something, now.

This wasn't fair! She didn't have a spell for stone! Stone was stubborn! Stone was not a living thing! She couldn't speak to it like a plant. She couldn't manipulate its movements the way she could water or wind. She panted, trying to catch her breath while the magma churned below her. Magma. Fable's eyes widened. Solid rock might not flow, but *liquid* rock sure did.

She closed her eyes and focused all her energy on the glowing pool. When she used the gale spell on the wind, she could direct air currents almost effortlessly with the slightest suggestion. Water took a little more effort, but her mother had insisted that they practice by the little stream near their clearing until Fable could control the flow in any direction, lifting the babbling stream into curling waves and spinning it into dancing eddies.

Magma was, as Fable had expected, many magnitudes harder. It took precious seconds just to lock her mind on the molten rock, but with tremendous effort, Fable felt it slowly responding. She let out a gasp of victory. She could do this.

235

The surface of the magma was the most resistant, but if Fable dug deeper, she could coax the flow from farther down, where it was hottest. It emerged in a dripping cone at first, and then a broad wave. It sank back to the surface when Fable allowed herself a moment to wipe the dripping sweat from her eyes, but she tried again, pressing on the wave with her mental hand as it rose until it flattened into a sheet of scorching yellow-orange.

Fable's whole body felt sunburned, and she was starting to get dizzy from the effort, but still she channeled the flow of the glowing magma with every ounce of energy left in her. The curtain of liquid rock swept around and around the broken pillar, red-hot and crackling, wrapping itself around the stone column like a bandage around a broken ankle. Heat poured off the structure in waves as Fable worked, and the cavern around her was beginning to feel like the inside of a furnace.

For one hopeful moment, the fragments of the crumbling pillar stopped shifting. Fable gulped a breath of hot, dry air and held on to the magma sheet as firmly as she could.

But then, with a series of angry *pops* as loud as cannon fire, the towering column shuddered and began to splinter again, broken shards striking Fable's blanket of lava as if it were nothing more than chewing gum wrapped around a snapping branch.

The cavern rocked. Huge boulders thundered down, blasting craters into the stone floor. The terrain around Fable was transforming from solid ground marked with patches of lava to a sea of lava marked with patches of solid ground. A spear of white light cut through the clouds above Fable, and she squinted against the sudden brightness. Her heart sank into her stomach. Daylight. If she was seeing daylight, the surface above them was cracking. That was bad. That was very bad.

"Rrraghh!" Fable growled. Sweat trickled down her neck. She could still feel the magma shifting in response to her invisible grasp, but even her fiercest magic couldn't hold it any tighter. It was still too fluid, too molten. At best she was delaying the inevitable. If only she could cool it back to solid rock. Maybe, if she hit it with one good burst of wind—but she would have to let go of the flow in order to cast gale, and without her holding the magma in place, the pillar would fall to pieces at once. Her head was pounding. Her chest ached. She couldn't catch her breath.

No. She couldn't give up—it couldn't be too late. *There is no such thing as too late for a queen.* But even a queen could need help. More than ever before, Fable needed her mother.

"Mama!" she cried aloud.

There was no sound in response but the grim crunching of the pillar giving way above her. And then, so gently that Fable thought she must be imagining it at first, the currents behind her shifted. Fable's curls blew forward around her eyes.

"I can't . . . do it . . . on my own!" she gasped, her every muscle screaming with the effort of maintaining the spell.

Fable held her breath. And then the air rippled with shadows. The hairs on the back of Fable's neck stood on end as an icy breeze swept past her, giving Fable a startling temporary respite from the inferno.

THEN WE WILL DO IT TOGETHER, said the Thing.

In another moment, the Thing was in the air. It fluttered over the chasm of lava, not gracefully like a bird, but clumsily, like a torn umbrella caught in a powerful wind. Still, it flew. The air around it wavered like the horizon on a summer's day, bending where the Thing's aura of cold met the magma's merciless heat. As it neared the pillar, the Thing sprawled itself out, wider and wider, every sliver of liquid blackness flattening and stretching until Fable could see the glow of the hot magma coming through its sinewy sheets of darkness.

And then it struck the pillar.

Shadows hissed and boiled as they touched the glowing rock, and glassy, soot-black bubbles blossomed across the surface. The Thing flinched and shed the boiling shadows from its leathery form, leaving them to sizzle where they stuck to the hot pillar—but it did not stop. It spun around and around the column, dropping shadow after shadow, literally throwing itself at the pillar piece by piece, until the glow began to fade from the stones. The Thing got smaller and the rock got darker, until soon, what remained of Fable's magma bandage looked like burnt, blackened treacle at the bottom of a ruined saucepan, and what remained of the Thing looked . . . small.

Fable cautiously released her mental grip. Her whole body was shaking and her head felt adrift, like at any moment it might float away. But the pillar held.

When the Thing was finally done, the last pitiful scrap of darkness tumbled out of the air. It turned and spun as it fell, no bigger than a tattered dish rag. Fable watched it, squinting her eyes against the heat and the steam, and she could have sworn she saw a living creature tucked within the scrap of shadows, like a mouse or a shrew—small and soft and frail.

Fable's vision blurred before she could see it land. There was an awful lot of ground in that direction that wasn't ground anymore. She swallowed. Her head was spinning, but the horrible clouds above her were lifting at last, venting out into the open air through the freshly broken cracks. The glistening shafts of white light piercing down from above danced in front of her. It was beautiful, in its own way, and it made Fable think that maybe—just maybe—the worst was over.

It was not.

"Whoa," said Joseph Burton. He put a hand over his brow to shield his eyes from the light filtering down through the dissipating mist. He and Cole had watched from the far side of the chamber as a sheet of magma had hardened around the crumbling central pillar. In the distance, at the center of the cavern, they could just make out Fable as she let her arms drop to her sides. "There's some magical magma witch holding the thing together!" said Joseph.

"I know her!" said Cole. "She's a friend of mine. Fable!"

Joseph looked down at Cole. "Do *I* know her?"

"Not yet," said Cole. "But you will. There are a lot of people you're going to meet."

"Cole!"

Cole spun at the sound of his brother's voice. "Tinn?"

"Cole!" Tinn came barreling across the broken ground, and the two of them collided in a spinning bear hug. "You're alive!"

"Tinn! I thought I lost you!"

"You did! But you found me again! Oof. Not quite so tight—it's been a rough day."

"Fair," said Cole. "Not over yet, either." They pulled apart, and Cole glanced back at Joseph. "I, um, I found someone else, too."

Tinn looked up, and his smile froze as he processed the man's features. He opened his mouth as if to speak, but it only hung there as the silence lengthened.

"No, it's fine." Evie's voice pierced the bubble of the moment. "I'll just carry the hero of the hour across this dangerous hellscape all by myself." She was slogging forward, a barely conscious Fable leaning heavily on her shoulders.

The boys hurried to help, taking over, one of them under each of Fable's arms.

Evie rotated her neck and stretched her shoulders. "Glad to see you, Cole." Her gaze landed on the strange, ragged man, and her eyes widened. "No way. Is this really . . . *him*?"

"I guess so," Joseph answered. His expression was straining, but he seemed to be holding on to a timid spark of comprehension now, against the currents of his fragile memory. He stared at Tinn, then Cole, then back again. "And I guess this means she kept it after all."

Tinn's eyes dropped to the floor.

Cole's mouth tightened.

"*Him*, not *it*," panted Fable, lifting her chin just a hair. She looked pale, but there was still a spark behind her eyes.

"Sorry," Joseph said. "She kept *him*. You. Both of you—because of course she did." He glanced back and forth one more time. "We were supposed to talk about it again when I got home. But I *knew* she had already made up her mind. I knew it. Which one of you—"

A piano-sized chunk of stone thundered down the slope not twenty feet from where they were standing and rumbled along the floor until it rolled over the crumbling edge and into the magma below.

"That's not important right now," said Cole. "What's important is finding Mom and getting everybody out of here."

Theolog Feldspar, Low Holy Underminer: second level, emerged from his chambers into the warm light of Delvers' Deep. They had done it. After countless generations and entire lifetimes of toil, they had finally done it. He was not certain when his sigil stone had ruptured, but he had hoped. Now, looking up to see the central pillar quaking and the floor cracking and crumbling away to reveal the sacred pool of the Ancient One, there was no question. He could not see the Low Priest from where he stood, but surely he must be nearby, basking in the glory of having realized every delver's destiny.

"It is time!" Theolog cried out. His brothers and sisters were peeking out from tunnels and caves as well, hoods thrown back to take in the glory of the end days. Some wore expressions of awe and excitement, but more looked wide-eyed and nervous. "Do not fear!" Theolog bellowed. "Remember that we are the chosen few! We alone will be spared by the great serpent in the coming days and rewarded generously for our unwavering devotion!" He beamed at his fellow delvers.

It was then that the floor shattered and Theolog was dropped unceremoniously into superheated magma. There was no scream. Before the Low Holy Underminer could know what was happening, he was a cinder.

A rippling arc of scales as broad as mattresses broke the surface beside Theolog's remains, sliding out of the magma and back in again.

There was a brief pause while the watching acolytes froze and weighed the options of becoming a faithful smudge on the scales of their god or appearing disloyal from a safe distance. Many of them arrived at the same mental arithmetic at the same moment, and the air filled with their panicked cries.

Cole squinted into the haze as dozens of figures with leathery ears and smooshed-in noses raced around frantically. Some of them wore humble shirts and trousers, a few had helmets like miners, and still more wore the red robes of the acolytes. The one thing they all shared was a matching expression of fear. They were like ants who had successfully tunneled into a kitchen only to find themselves caught in the baking oven. On the far wall, Cole spotted Tommy pushing his way onto an already overcrowded elevator. Those who could not make it on before the lift began to rise hurried to join the throng already pouring up the stairs to the second level and into a hole in the cavern wall.

"They are right to run," said a voice beside the kids. Cole spun. The woman standing there was dressed in gray, her hair pulled back behind her head. "As would *you* be."

"We *can't*," Fable told her, raising her voice over the gurgling crackle of the pool.

"Sure you can," said Madam Root. "With me."

"We need to get the prisoners out first," said Cole.

Madam Root shook her head. "The Low Order have at least a hundred mindless servants, child. I cannot save them all—and you certainly can't. But I *might* be able to save you, if you stop dawdling. Come on."

"Not without my mama," said Fable. "Or Annie, or

244

Nudd, or . . . the old cranky one whose name I can't remember right now. We're not leaving *any* of them behind."

Madam Root sighed. "Suit yourself. Without me you have only two ways to get out of here."

A loud clanging rang across the cavern. Soon after came the piercing squeal of twisting metal, accompanied by a dozen more squeals that sounded decidedly more like voices. Cole turned in time to see a towering steel track tear free from the wall and hit the magma pool with a ruby splash before sinking beneath the fiery surface.

"Make that *one* way," said Madam Root. "It seems the delvers' lift is out of commission."

Cole swallowed.

"The Cardinal Channel is your last option." Madam Root pointed to the opening on the landing above them. The last straggling delvers were just disappearing through the mouth of the tunnel. "You have a long climb ahead of you. I sincerely hope it does not collapse before you reach the top." And with those bracing words of encouragement, she stepped back and sank smoothly into the solid wall of the cavern.

"Come on," Cole said. "We can't stop now. Which way do we go?"

Joseph looked at him blankly. "Who, me? Why? Where are we going?"

"Ugh!" Cole groaned. "The prisoners! We're freeing the prisoners!"

"Are we?" Joseph brightened. "Good for us! Believe it or not, I was a prisoner here for just a little while, but I got away."

"Which way?" Cole snapped.

"Right. Sorry. The prisoners' barracks are just ahead."

Debris rained down around them as they raced toward a cave opening along the wall of the cavern.

"Are you sure?" called Evie. "There are no bars or locks or anything."

"Why would they need locks?" Joseph answered.

Cole poked his head through the door.

The woman in gray had been right: at least a hundred people lay within—trolls, gnomes, hobs, and a motley assortment of other captive workers waited within the barracks, their bodies resting on spartan slabs of stone. Cole might have thought he had entered a morgue, except he could see their chests rising and falling. Many of them had their eyes open, staring blankly at the ceiling.

Tinn pushed in beside him. "Mom?" Tinn called. "Are you in here?"

No response.

Fable made her way into the chamber, her eyes sweeping from bed to bed.

"Uncle Jim!" Evie cried. She hurried to the side of one of the slabs. "Uncle Jim, it's me!" The old man was lying prone. His eyes half opened at the sound of her voice, but he gave no further sign of recognition.

"Give him some bitterwort!" called Cole.

Evie patted her vest, but her fingers froze on the tattered fabric where a pocket used to be. She shook her head. "No good. All my herbs were on the side that got sandpapered along a cavern wall."

"You're all free now!" Tinn yelled. "You can go!"

One or two of the slumped figures turned their heads lazily to stare in the twins' general direction. None of them made any indication that they might care to move.

"Why are you all just lying here? You're in danger!" Tinn yelled. "The cavern is collapsing, and there's a giant lava snake about to flood this whole place!"

None of them moved.

"Annie!" As one, Tinn and Cole turned to see Joseph standing over their mother. His hand shook as he brushed a hair out of her face. "Can you hear me?"

Annie did not react.

"I know you're in there." Joseph gave her hand a gentle squeeze. When he let go, her hand slid lifelessly back to the slab.

Cole felt a cold lump growing in his stomach. His

mother's chest rose and fell, but she wasn't showing any signs of stirring.

"We're running out of time," said Tinn.

Joseph leaned down—and for a moment Cole was reminded of Sleeping Beauty waking to true love's kiss. His father pressed his temple tenderly against his mother's, his lips close to her ear. "We need you," he whispered. "Your boys need you. Come on. Wake up."

Annie Burton sat up.

Cole's heart lurched.

Joseph nearly fell over backward. He steadied himself and looked his wife in the eyes. "Annie?"

Her gaze remained unfocused, and she swayed slightly where she sat. She was upright and technically conscious— but if she recognized the man in front of her, she gave no indication.

Cole could remember what it felt like, pulling himself out of the trance. Everything had been so muddy and confusing. It had been so much easier to simply do as he was told. "That fog," he said. "It's got Oddmire water and fin-folk weed in it. She can't think for herself. None of them can. Try giving her clear, simple directions."

Joseph nodded. "Right," he said. "Stand up!"

Annie Burton swung her feet to the side and stood.

Joseph clapped his hands in excitement. "It's working! She's listening!"

The cavern shuddered, and a chunk of stone clattered from the ceiling.

"Let's see if we can get it working faster," said Cole. He climbed up on top of an empty bed and cupped his hands on either side of his mouth. "Hey, everybody! Walk out that door and up the stairs! Right now! Go!"

As one, the huge crowd of prisoners stood and shambled like zombies toward the door and out into the heat of the main cavern. Satyrs and gnomes and trolls bumped and bumbled their way to the stony stairs and began to climb.

Tinn spotted Nudd and patted him on the shoulder as he passed. It was hard to see the indomitable High Chief of the horde looking so lifeless and docile. Near the middle of the procession, a woman draped in a bearskin cloak shuffled past.

"Mama!" Fable pushed through the shambling bodies to get to her mother. Raina's eyes were half-lidded, and she did not even turn to acknowledge her daughter. "It's okay, Mama," Fable said. "We're gonna get you out of here."

"That's the last of them!" Cole called out a minute later from the back of the world's most lackluster parade.

The end of the procession was halfway up the stairs when a flash of orange light and a wave of heat washed over them. In the middle of the cavern, what was left of the floor was giving way; baseball field–sized pieces of ground were breaking off and sinking into the heat of the glowing magma. Beneath the red-hot surface, the great serpent slid and swam, its scales glowing yellow-hot where they neared the open air.

"I don't have it in me to wrestle with lava again," said Fable. "We need to get out of here fast."

Tinn couldn't tell if the lone pillar in the center of the cavern was trembling again or if it was merely his vision dancing in the haze of heat. Either way, he didn't like to think about what was going to happen as soon as that enormous snake decided to grind its lava body directly against the column.

The ground shuddered, and Tinn nearly lost his balance. The head of the procession had almost reached the exit. They would be out soon—but too many shakes like that before they made it, and they were sure to lose somebody over the edge and into the lava below. In the back of his mind he heard a noise like the distant rumble of thunder. He glanced up.

The quake had knocked loose a pair of boulders as

big as tool sheds, and they were now rolling and rumbling down the incline and headed straight toward them.

"Fable!" he yelled. "Do something!"

Fable's eyes were wide. She drew a deep breath of dry, scorching air and poured all of her energy into the spell. "Gale!" The hot air rising off of the magma pool blasted upward with the force of a giant's punch. Several of the prisoners stumbled off their feet as the gust collided with the boulders, blasting them off course to the left and right.

Fable's knees buckled and her eyes rolled back. She hit the ground with a thump so soft it could not possibly have been heard over the crash of the stairway being smashed into pebbles.

The whole landing shuddered, and Annie, still shuffling near the back of the crowd, lost her footing. The crumbling stair she was standing on fell away, and she tipped backward. Cole screamed, and Joseph dove toward the ledge, hands outstretched.

Tinn spun his head to see what was happening, but a gaggle of brain-dead former prisoners blocked his view. He edged his way, as quickly as he dared, back through the crowd just as Joseph and Cole together hauled Annie up the last of the unbroken stairs and onto the even landing.

"Thanks, kid," Joseph said to Cole. "If you happen to mention any of my dashing heroics to your mother when she comes out of it, feel free to leave out the part where I rattled her head against the stairs and almost dropped her twice."

"Given that the alternative was a fiery death," said Cole, "I think she'd probably let it slide this time."

"Hey," Evie called from up ahead. "We've got another problem."

Tinn leaned around the masses to see what she was talking about. Up ahead, the parade had stopped. Although the other boulder had missed the front of the procession, it had slammed onto the landing ahead of them, wedging itself squarely in front of the cave mouth. Their one escape—the Cardinal Channel—was completely blocked.

TWENTY-SEVEN

EVEN WITH JOSEPH, THE TWINS, AND EVIE ALL pushing together, the boulder did not wobble. As they struggled, a strange, deep hum reverberated through the cavern. It carried with it emotions: a mournful sense of isolation and intense loneliness. Cole stopped pushing, and his eyes met his father's. He saw, behind the welling sadness, a growing glimmer of real recognition.

"Do you remember who I am?" said Cole.

"I think so," said Joseph. He took a deep breath and reached a hand up to rub his chin. He seemed startled for a second to find a matted beard there, but then looked back at Cole. "You got real big," he said. "But . . . you're my son, aren't you?"

"One of them," said Cole.

Joseph looked confused, and Cole nodded to Tinn. Joseph turned, then looked from Tinn to Cole and back again.

"She kept it," he mumbled. "Right."

Tinn's shoulders sagged. "Yeah," he managed. "She kept me." He plodded away, not that there was very far for him to go. He sat, despondent, on the edge of the landing. Thirty feet below, the magma bulged and crackled.

After a few moments, Joseph Burton sat down beside him.

"Hey, kid," said the man.

Tinn didn't look at him. "You remember who *I* am?"

"I remember," said Joseph.

They sat in silence for a moment. Behind them, Cole scrabbled at the top of the boulder, trying in vain to figure out a way over it. Evie had gone to sit with Fable's head in her lap, fanning her friend in an effort to revive her. Everything had fallen apart, and Tinn wanted nothing more than to hear his mother's comforting voice, to feel her fingers ruffle his hair. His mother would know what to say to make him feel better. She always did.

"So," said Joseph. "What's it like, being a changeling?"

"It's not something you really think about," grumbled Tinn.

"Stupid question. It's all strange to me. Just trying to wrap my head around it." Joseph flicked a bit of debris into the fiery pit below. "Do you remember impersonating Thomas for the first time?"

"His name is Cole—and I was a *baby.*"

"Right. Of course. But you kept up the act all this time? Why?"

Tinn looked up at the man. He was watching Tinn closely, like an appraiser taking in the detailed brush strokes of a forgery. "It wasn't an *act*," Tinn answered. "It was my *life*. It was the only life I knew. I couldn't even control it until recently."

"Sorry. That was rude, wasn't it? I'm just curious. I don't know anything about you. Not really."

Tinn shrugged. "I get it. It's weird."

"I'm not sure how much you know about me, but if you'd like—"

"I know you wanted to get rid of me." Tinn hadn't meant to say it out loud, but once it was out there, he couldn't find it in himself to regret it.

Joseph sighed. "It's true," he said. "I did. We didn't know what you were. We didn't even know which one you were. The fact that there were two of you was new and odd, and I didn't know what to do. I was worried for my son. I wanted to protect my family from a scary . . . from what I *thought* was a scary creature. I didn't know any better."

Tinn stared at the ground. His chest felt tight.

"But you know what? For a goblin, you seem like a pretty good kid after all."

Tinn's stomach turned. "Don't do that," he said.

"I didn't mean any—"

"Being a goblin doesn't define me. Neither does being a human. I am who I am because of the people who were always there for me—there for *us*." His ears felt hot and he clenched his hands into fists. "When you *weren't*."

Joseph looked Tinn in the eyes. "I can see that," he said, softly. "You have a lot of your mother in you. You kids were lucky to have her. And she was lucky to have you. *Both* of you."

Tinn turned his face away. He hated how Joseph looked at him. It still felt like the man was searching for the flaw in Tinn's disguise—for the seam in his mask. Tinn stood on the edge of the rocks, looking down over the desolate, boiling scene below.

Through the haze of heat, he could make out the magma serpent's golden scales sliding through the liquid rock. Chunks of solid stone had broken off and were drifting around it on the surface of the burning lake like wretched little islands. A flutter of movement caught his eye—a feeble patch of darkness in the sea of orange light.

"I'm doing this all wrong," Joseph said behind him. "But for what it's worth, kid, I *don't* wish that I had gotten rid of you," said Joseph. "I wish that I had gotten . . . to be one of those somebodies who was always there for you."

Tinn swallowed hard. He nodded. "You want to be there for some scary creature you used to think was your enemy?" He turned and met Joseph's eyes.

"I really do," said Joseph.

Tinn took a deep breath. "Well then," he said, "I guess I am like you a little bit after all."

And then Tinn leapt off the ledge.

The Thing dug itself as deeply as it could into its last wilting scrap of a shadow like a shrew cowering under a leaf, but there was no escaping the heat. The Thing had given everything it had to help the witchy child, and still the cavern trembled and the magma crept steadily over the side of the rocky island. It wouldn't be long now. And it was going to hurt.

The Thing had pondered death many times. Mostly, it had pondered someone else's death, often hungrily—but it *had* thought about its own death, too. It had imagined painful deaths and lingering deaths, but this time the Thing's mind caught stubbornly on a new thought. The Thing had never pondered a *good* death.

The changeling, Tinn, was alive because of the Thing. The child had said *thank you*. The boy's friends would also live, thanks to the Thing—and their survival would make the boy's life happier. The Thing's sacrifice had made all that possible. It *was* going to die, and yet . . . it felt *good*. It had been prepared for death, but it had not been prepared for a death that *meant something*.

For the first time the Thing could remember, it felt full—the terrible hunger that usually raged inside of it had been somehow sated. As the last of the shadow finally boiled away to smoke, it felt content in a way it had never known before. If the Thing's *death* meant something, it mused, then some part of its *life* must have meant something, too. And perhaps that was enough.

The air above the magma lake rippled with heat. Defenseless, powerless, the Thing stared, numbly, as the golden haze danced and wobbled before it. It could almost imagine the shape of a mighty eagle in midair, swooping toward it, wings outstretched. The Thing blinked and wobbled where it stood. Was this death, coming for it at last? Or just a mirage? The eagle grew larger as it neared, and soon the Thing could make out the curve of the sharp beak, the texture of each quivering feather, the curve of the talons, outstretched and reaching.

Tinn had hoped maintaining his bird form might be simpler without the befuddling mists of the Oddmire to throw him off, but nothing about this felt simple. He flapped hard the moment he felt the Thing's meager weight in his talons. Coasting downward had been much easier than rising, but now he had to go up. The scorching air pouring off of the magma provided some lift—which Tinn used to the best of his limited abilities, but the heat was still unbearable. Eagles were not meant to fly under these conditions—*nothing* was meant to survive in this place. Except, it seemed, for the coiled colossus now waking up beneath them.

A spray of magma spewed up as another chunk of falling debris hit the surface. Tinn pulled the Thing close to his feathery chest. It was like hugging an ice cube, which— under the circumstances—was at least a small comfort. Today had taken more strange turns than Tinn could have possibly imagined. What used to be his right arm exploded with pain, and Tinn lurched to one side before getting his flight clumsily back under control. He surveyed the damage as best he could mid-flight. A few glowing beads of liquid rock had spattered his wing, and now the feathers were darkening around those spots and flickering with blossoming flames.

YOU ARE ON FIRE, said a voice from beneath Tinn.

Tinn tucked his head down and shot the Thing a withering glare over his beak.

I JUST THOUGHT YOU OUGHT TO KNOW, said the Thing.

Tinn brought his head up and pushed through the pain as hard as he could. The ledge was thirty feet ahead of them, but still too high. He could see his brother's face, pale with panic, and Evie's, too. They were yelling something and reaching out their hands. Tinn strained to climb higher on the sweltering breeze, but the pain was blinding. With every pump of his wings, he was losing altitude. He needed to climb higher.

YOU WILL RISE MORE EASILY WITHOUT ME.

Tinn ignored the voice. Twenty feet away. He wasn't nearly high enough. He wasn't going to make it, and dropping the Thing's puny weight would not change that. His wing was too badly hurt.

YOU CANNOT SAVE US BOTH. RELEASE ME.

Ten feet. And falling. With his brother's outstretched hands tantalizingly close, Tinn gave one final tortured push and then tucked his wings back and spun upside down, opening his talons at the last second so the Thing whipped out of his grasp like a skipping stone.

Tinn smiled. *Think fast.* The tiny creature twirled wildly through the air . . . and into Cole's startled hands.

And then Tinn fell.

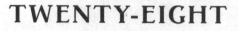

TWENTY-EIGHT

THE THING DID NOT SEND ICY SHIVERS THROUGH Cole's bones the way it once had, but it still felt like he had caught a dead mouse. Its sickly body was damp and oddly cool in spite of the oppressive heat all around them. Cole dropped the Thing at his feet and did not even bother to watch as it scampered away—he was too busy staring numbly as the eagle that was his brother tumbled backward toward a lake of molten magma.

Cole's voice cracked as he screamed, "Tinn!"

The earth shook, and before Cole could make sense of what was happening, he felt a broad arm hook around his waist and haul him off his feet. He hit the ground just as an avalanche of stones came thundering down on the ledge where he had just been standing. Joseph held his body over Cole like a human umbrella until he was satisfied that the rockslide was done.

"What happened?" asked Evie. "Where's Tinn?"

Cole hurried back to peer over the ledge. The glowing surface of the magma rippled with a dozen fresh dark spots. Any one of them could be . . . "I-I can't see him," Cole breathed. "He's gone."

Joseph put a hand on Cole's shoulder. "He's a changeling, right? Maybe he changed himself into something tiny. Like a spider. He's probably climbing the cliff wall right now with eight little legs."

"It . . . it doesn't work like that," Cole managed. "It's all the same *him* on the inside, just squished around into different shapes."

Joseph took a deep breath. "I'm so sorry, kid. I really am. But we need to keep moving. We need to find a way out."

"Our way out is on the other side of that boulder that none of us can move," Evie said. "Or on the other side of that lake of lava, if you prefer."

"Right," Joseph sighed. "We're between a rock and a hard place, except the *hard place* is molten death."

"Ugh." Fable grunted as she lifted her head. "What's happening? Am I dead yet?"

"Not yet," said Evie, holding Fable steady as she tried to sit up. "But not for lack of trying."

"Glad you're back with us," said Joseph. "We need to move that big rock over there to get everybody out of here. Think you can use some of that magic of yours on it?"

Fable shook her head, and the subtle motion nearly threw her off-balance. "Sorry," she grunted. "Not my area. Rocks don't listen to my magic." She rubbed her head with one hand and leaned on Evie for support with the other. "Which is super annoying, because the stupid kobolds can magic their way through them just fine."

"What was that?" said Joseph.

"The kobolds," Fable repeated. "They can . . ." With great effort she raised her chin and looked up. "They can move through solid stone. The kobolds could get us out."

A hundred feet off, a barrage of falling rocks whistled through the air and splashed into the magma below with a series of heavy slaps, followed by a gurgling hiss.

"The kobolds left," mumbled Cole. He was still staring down into the pool, the orange light reflecting in his eyes. "They ran away. We're on our own."

"We can call them back," said Fable.

"Do you know how to talk to those things?" said Joseph.

"Not exactly," said Fable. "I know they're smart, though. They did things on command for Madam Root."

"And Madam Root is . . . ?" asked Joseph.

"Not . . . here," admitted Fable.

"It's no good," murmured Cole. "Nobody is coming to save us this time."

"Well, we have to try something!" barked Fable. "Why are you acting like this?"

Fable's eyes were scowling as they met Cole's. His were tired and red and rimmed with tears.

"Wait," said Fable. "Where's Tinn?"

Cole let his chin sag down to his chest.

"Where's Tinn?" Fable repeated. She turned to Joseph, who shook his head soberly.

"Oh." Fable swallowed.

"I can do it," said Evie, softly.

They all turned their attention to her as she fumbled with one of the pockets in her vest.

"I can call the kobolds," she said. With shaking hands, she produced a tiny purple vial. "It's magic from the spriggans to let me talk to any animal. I can call them back. I'll only get one shot, though."

Below them, the body of the impossibly huge serpent broke the surface again, glowing white-hot, moving faster as it uncoiled. It was like watching a mountain of light unfolding beneath them. The scales skidded against the central pillar's foundation, sending a spray of ruby droplets splattering all around it. The surface of the yawning magma lake swelled and rose as the Ancient One unfurled. Already the glowing, liquid rock had completely swallowed the last crumbling remnants of the charred floor and begun to climb higher up the walls of the cavern.

"It's no good," sighed Cole. "Even if you did call the kobolds back—even if a few of them heard you and tried to help—there's just too many of us."

Fable glanced over at her mother and all the rest of the freed captives, who remained blank and expressionless while the world crumbled around them. "Then we'll take turns," Fable said. "It's better than just sitting here waiting for another rock to land on our heads."

Evie nodded and tipped her head back as she downed the vial in a single gulp. She gave a little shiver like she had just felt a jolt of static electricity, and then she stepped closer to the wall of the cavern and took a deep breath.

"And then what?" Cole went on, grimly. "We make it to the other side of a rock? We'd still be lost in the dark, still buried miles beneath the surface."

Evie hesitated a moment, worry drawn across her face—but then she leaned in and let her forehead rest directly on the stone as she called out in her loudest voice. What emerged from her mouth was not language in any human tongue, nor any of the typical sounds that animals are supposed to make. It droned and hiccuped in a series of discordant tones. When she was through, she repeated the same series of strange sounds, cupping her hands around her mouth as she did.

"The delvers weren't digging themselves a temple down here," Cole went on. "They were digging us a grave."

"Oh, stop it!" Fable shouted. "I get it! He's gone! He's gone, and that hurts so bad I wanna be sick, and I can't imagine how much more it hurts for you." She took a slow, deep breath. "But we need to keep trying! Do you really think Tinn would want to be the reason that *you* just gave up? Tinn would *want* you to keep going. Tinn would want you to be the hero for all of them that you always were for him."

Cole said nothing. The tears that had been welling up in his eyes finally slid down his cheeks, leaving trails in the soot. He did not reach up to wipe them away.

SHE IS WRONG, said a voice on the wind. It was frail and breathy, but Cole could hear it as clearly as if it were whispering directly in his ear. From behind a cracked lump of rock, the Thing's tiny head emerged.

"Shut up," Cole growled. His fists clenched. He could feel the chasm of pain and helplessness into which he had been sinking suddenly turning to anger. Rage rose in him like a fire climbing a hayloft. "You don't get to have a say in this right now," he snarled through clenched teeth.

BUT—

"I said *shut up*! Tinn trusted you! You tore him down, you tried to *kill* him, and he *still* felt bad for you! He *saved* you! Now he hasn't been gone five minutes, and you're already tearing *me* down? You want me to just give up and die? What is *wrong* with you?"

QUITE A LOT, said the Thing. BUT SHE IS STILL WRONG.

"I said shut—"

BECAUSE THE CHANGELING IS NOT DEAD. I CAN FEEL HIM.

The Thing's next words were drowned out by a sudden, deafening, sucking sound from the lake below. A blinding light illuminated the whole cavern as the serpent's head finally broke the surface of the magma. Whole cow fields could have rested on the flat of the creature's head— not that they could have rested there long without being reduced to ashes. It hurt Cole's eyes to look directly at the brilliant glow for too long. As the colossal serpent rose, so, too, did the bubbling magma lake. The whole cavern shuddered again, and this time it did not stop.

"Holy heck," Fable breathed. "Now would be a really good time for some kobolds to start showing up." Golden light washed over them as the snake's sun-white eyes blinked open in front of them. It rose, the air around it rippling in a wobbly haze.

"I didn't call the kobolds," Evie stammered, transfixed as the behemoth slid higher and higher in front of her. The heat radiating off of the serpent washed over them in waves like an invisible incoming tide. Still, the cavern rumbled and shook all around them.

Somewhere, high above, a thunderous crash announced yet another onslaught of rocks shaken loose by the shuddering earth. Piano-sized stones came tumbling down the slope of the cave, bouncing and spinning and colliding with heavy *cracks* and *bangs*, bound toward the crowd of freed prisoners.

Annie Burton and Raina stood beside each other at the front of the pack, their expressions placid and their eyes dull.

"Nooo!" Cole could not hear his own voice—all sound melted into a meaningless cacophony—but he felt the scream of horror leave his body. It was as if time slowed down and he was frozen in place, helplessly watching it all unfold in front of him.

The magma rose below them. The rocks thundered down from above. The serpent had turned its fiery eyes toward the crowd. And then the rocks on the side of the cavern rippled like the surface of a lake in a soft breeze. A moment later, a monstrous animal with bristly fur and a frame like a locomotive burst free from the solid stone, its mouth yawning so wide it could have fit an entire mail cart, complete with horses, on its tongue. Its teeth were as big as whiskey barrels and looked as if they could grind mountains into molehills. The kobb scooped up a dozen bodies with one swoop of its mighty jaws. Former prisoners tumbled over one another into a pile on the kobb's tongue, Raina and Annie at the top of the heap. Cole watched, horrified, as the monster prepared to devour them in the moments before the magma or the serpent could reach them.

"They came! Yes!" Evie yelled beside him. "Hey! Listen up! Everybody grab on to the kobb!" Her voice, full of urgent authority, cut through the air like a bell.

Glassy-eyed goblins, slack-jawed gnomes, and tottering trolls all obeyed the instruction mindlessly. Those within reach clutched handfuls of bristly hair and then lurched off their feet as the kobb kept plowing forward. By the time the beast plunged back into the wall of the cavern, it had thirty or more bodies clinging to its sides, plus the dozen it had snatched up in its mouth.

The stones in its wake had not stopped rippling before two more kobbs came diving out of the rocky walls farther down. These beasts echoed the movements of the first, scooping up mouthfuls of freed prisoners and collecting the rest on their backs just seconds before the ledge they had been standing on was obliterated by the landslide. The swelling magma hungrily consumed the debris. The snake's mighty head merely turned to follow the frantic exodus.

Cole barely had time to snap out of his astonishment and grab on himself as the last lumbering beast raced past them. The creature's furry coat was layered thickly over muscles as wide as barn walls, and Cole rose and fell with each loping stride. The fur in his hands felt like a horse's mane, but it was dense and long enough that Cole could wrap it once around his hands for a firmer grip. The kobb smelled a bit like a horse too, musky and earthy.

Cole pulled his knees up under him as the ground whipped away beneath them. He glanced from side to side. Fable had taken hold on his left and Evie on his right. He could see his father over Evie's shoulder—that was good— but had they left somebody behind? It had all happened so quickly. Had everyone heard Evie's command? Had they all grabbed hold? Too late for stragglers now.

Cole glanced over his shoulder for one last look at the hellish underground cavern before the kobb leapt toward the far wall.

The changeling is not dead. The Thing had said so. It said it could *feel* him. Tinn was still alive . . . which meant he was still trapped in the cavern somewhere!

"*Wait—*" Cole said.

But then the stones enveloped them, sound abruptly cut to silence, and the whole world was a sea of warm molasses.

TWENTY-NINE

THE SERPENT ROSE OUT OF THE LIQUID ROCK, its song a ballad of aching loneliness. There had been more of its kind, in the beginning. The earth had been hot then, and there had been such beautiful fires everywhere. The serpent missed the world as it used to be. It hardly recognized the world any longer. It could hear sounds on the distant surface—but they were wrong sounds, foreign, alien sounds. They were the songs of creatures who knew nothing of the sweet aroma of molten metals or the tender embrace of a blazing fire. But perhaps they *could* know. Perhaps the earth could be as it once was. The serpent could set the world ablaze—the whole world—a paradise of fire and ash. *For all of them.*

A column of rock rose high into the air, precisely as the serpent had dreamt it for eons. It knew this scene. It had seen it play out countless times as it slept. The pillar would crumble, the land above would fall, and then the serpent would rise to make the world right. Yes. It was time to make real the visions it had dreamt. The serpent turned its head toward the pillar. How very little it would take to snap the feeble column.

In the space between the serpent and the pillar, the magma bubbled.

The serpent paused.

Something was rising above the glowing surface. The serpent lowered its white-hot head to better see the tiny shape rising out of the liquid rock.

It was—impossibly—another serpent. Miniature scales of brilliant gold dripped with crackling lava. The tiny creature was a fraction of the great serpent's size, but it was unmistakably kin and kind.

The serpent felt welling emotions wash over it. With infinite gentleness, it lowered its tremendous head until it was inches away from its tiny counterpart, and then it sang. The little snake pressed its glowing head against the great serpent's snout.

274

Tinn had not had much time to react as he was falling out of the air. The magma had been rushing toward him, his wing had been on fire, and so he had allowed instinct to take over. He had been sure, at first, that he had failed—but then the magma had begun to slide beneath his serpentine body like warm mud. It stung, but like the sting of a hot bath after a long day in the snow—and the longer he spun through the glowing pool, the more the warmth of it soothed him. The part of him that had been burning feathers only moments before still throbbed, but the heat was now soaking the pain away, bit by bit.

The great serpent's head was wider than the town square back in Endsborough. It took up almost all of Tinn's vision as it neared, glowing white-hot. Tinn felt a surge of tentative joy as the serpent crooned. In its song, Tinn could hear a lifetime of loneliness and a glowing beacon of trembling, reckless hope.

Tinn stretched his serpentine body forward and pressed his own scaly head against the beast's. The great serpent hummed, deep and quavering, and Tinn could feel the creature's mournful relief, almost unbearable in its intensity. He steeled himself against the flood of emotions. He could not afford to lose focus and accidentally transform back—not here, not now.

Another deep hum, and Tinn felt himself wrapped in

a warm future. The sky above would be smoke black and the whole earth would glow like a beautiful ember. Tinn closed his eyes as the longing filled him. It would be a perfect world. For both of them. Together. Tinn found himself wanting that more than anything.

Remembering himself, who he was on the inside, felt like swimming upstream—but Tinn was there, under the heavy blanket of the serpent's song. He felt the serpent's thoughts so powerfully that he thought his skull might burst, but if the Ancient One could communicate this way, then so could Tinn. Tentatively, he opened his mouth and warbled a reply.

There were no words, but Tinn willed his own feelings back toward the serpent as he crooned. He imagined Fable and the queen, trying desperately to save their forest. He imagined Evie, feet pounding across the rocks as she raced to escape a painful death, and he imagined Kull, beside himself with worry back at the horde. He imagined his mother and Cole, somehow free of the whole mess, waiting for him back in their cozy house, a fat old cat rubbing against their legs. Tinn imagined *home*.

The serpent pulled away. Tinn could feel its confusion.

Strange images danced through the serpent's mind. It saw creatures crawling across the face of the earth, ugly, hairy things, fleshy beasts draped in flimsy fabrics, hunkering in shelters of wood and plaster. They were like insects, an infestation, a blight to be purged from the serpent's perfect world—and yet . . .

It turned its head to look again at the young snake squirming in the magma in front of it. Its song was clumsy and inelegant, but it was so plaintive and urgent.

The mighty serpent closed its eyes. Humans hung in its mind. Hundreds of them. Thousands. Millions, all across the planet. It saw something else, too, behind their mushy skin and all that unsightly hair. It saw kindness. It saw passion and curiosity and creativity. Within these grotesque creatures, the serpent saw a capacity for such beauty and love. It shook its head and pulled back.

Countless beings had come and gone in the time the serpent had slumbered. Their lives were small and insignificant.

The little snake persisted, its feeble trill getting louder.

The serpent's vision widened. Somewhere, high above them, a proud mother horse was watching her foal trot for the first time on gangly legs. Across the forest, goblins were banding together, hand in hand, to repair a ruptured bridge. Pixies were darting through the air for the pure joy of the wind in their faces. Trolls and nymphs, wolves and deer, bats and bumblebees, and countless other creatures were living countless lives that the serpent could never fully comprehend. They were so different, so bizarre, and yet knowing that they were safe and well—for the moment— gave the serpent a warm sense of contentment. It allowed the feeling to settle over itself like a soft blanket.

And then a dark future opened up. The ground would crumble and the sky would be choked by ash and smoke. The serpent cringed as it felt the pangs of fear and pain. So many lives would be destroyed. Not one world, but a billion would burn, because each of those lives experienced its own world every day. The world of the peaceful tortoise and the world of the hurried bumblebee would vanish. The world of the gnomish inventor and the world of the goblin changeling— all of them would become one world, a world of death. And that world would be the serpent's and the serpent's alone.

The miniature snake's song tapered off, and the cavern fell silent once more.

The domed ceiling of the underground cavern was splintered with cracks, like the inside of an egg that had begun to hatch. Sunlight trickled down on them in glittering spears. The pillar in front of the serpent trembled under the weight of it all. It would not hold for long.

Tinn felt his head swim. He could not maintain a fire-snake form much longer. The heat was starting to burn again, slow and fierce, a sharp pain in the pit of his stomach that spread slowly out into his muscles and joints.

The magma swelled beneath Tinn as the giant serpent's head dipped beneath the surface, sending slow ripples across the glowing lake. In another moment, Tinn felt himself rising. The serpent's enormous head breached the surface like a whale, coming up directly under Tinn. He could only watch as thousands of feet of cavern walls slid past him in a blur.

The serpent tipped its snout, and Tinn began to slide off. He slithered and spun against the incline, but there was little he could do to keep himself from falling. He needn't have worried—no sooner had he tumbled away from the glowing Ancient One than he found himself landing in a heap on the floor of a high ledge. Once it had deposited the little snake, the great serpent ducked its head again and slid back down into the depths.

Tinn finally let go. His scales melted together into smooth skin and his bones shifted. His whole body felt like it was on fire, and he gasped for air, but it lasted for only a moment. Soon his arms were arms, his legs were legs, and

Tinn was himself again. He lay on his back for a long time, panting.

His arm stung. Angry red blisters were splattered across his elbow, right where his wing had caught the lava droplets. It sent ripples of pain up to his shoulder blades when he tried to bend it. With all the effort he could muster, he managed to roll himself over and crawl to the edge of the landing.

Far below, the serpent was spinning around the edges of the cavern, coiling higher and higher on itself like a giant golden spring. As it circled, its brilliant scales pulsed with heat, and the magma rose with it. The surface surged, flooding up the chamber until it had climbed ten stories, and then it paused.

With dread, Tinn turned his attention to the central column. The magma flow had completely enveloped the base of the pillar, and Tinn was sure it was going to finally crack—but before it could crumble under the heat, something peculiar happened. The surface of the lake darkened. It was bright orange one moment, and then, right before his eyes, it cooled to a dull red, black spots formed as it hardened, and in another minute, the whole enormous layer was dark, solid stone, encircled by a golden ring.

The serpent repeated its action, coiling higher and higher along the edge of the cavern, fresh crimson lava flooding out around its scales as it rose, spilling onto the newly hardened surface until the whole floor had become another deep lake of molten ruby rock. Then, once more, the serpent paused and the new layer cooled to solid stone. With each new layer, the cavern shrank, the floor rising slowly toward the roof.

Tinn let out a laugh. The serpent wasn't destroying the last of the supports, it was reinforcing them. In minutes, it was undoing countless generations of delvers' efforts by filling in the entire cave with solid stone. Endsborough and the Wild Wood would soon be resting on a bedrock foundation.

With that happy thought, Tinn tried to push himself up to standing. If he didn't want to become a part of that bedrock, he needed to get moving. There was still a lot of cavern between him and the surface, and he would have to find a way to climb it before the serpent caught up to him. He leaned on his bad arm for just a moment, and his vision swam with the pain. Shakily, he made it to his feet—but his legs felt like saltwater taffy and he collapsed back to his knees almost at once. He panted and tried hard not to pass out.

"How did you do it?" said a voice from behind him.

Tinn craned his neck to see a woman clad in a long gray dress. A bristling kobold was perched on her shoulders and another half a dozen circled her feet.

"I'm a changeling," Tinn said. "It's goblin magic. I can become . . . other things. For a little while."

"Not that," Madam Root said. "Impressive, but not what I mean. What I want to know is how you changed the serpent." She gestured down at the rising glow. "That creature has dreamt of nothing but the destruction of this world for longer than any of us has been alive. And yet, in a matter of minutes, you managed to convince it that a single village of insignificant humans was worth giving up its destiny?"

"I don't think it wanted to destroy anything," said Tinn. "Not really. And I'm not sure I believe in destiny at all."

"The delvers believed. They believed in a serpent at the end of the world, and they believed it with everything they were. They believed so hard that they very nearly made it a reality."

"Believing something doesn't make it true."

"Doesn't it?" Madam Root raised an eyebrow. "Well, believe it or not, that serpent would have burned everything you love to ashes."

"Maybe." Tinn shrugged. "But I don't think the serpent wanted to destroy anything, not really. It just wanted things to go back to the way they were." He took a deep breath. "It's hard when your whole world changes."

Madam Root eyed him.

"You are either very wise or very lucky, changeling."

Tinn shook his head. "I've nearly gotten myself killed half a dozen times in the past year alone. I feel like a walking bruise right now, and I'm pretty sure I'm going to get burned to a crisp in a few minutes."

Madam Root chuckled softly. "And yet, after everything you've been through, you still believe you can find good inside every monster you meet?"

"After everything I've been through," said Tinn, "I guess I don't believe in the monster part. But yeah, I believe in the good."

Madam Root nodded in silent approval.

Below them, the serpent continued to rise, a hundred feet at a time, the heat of its efforts preceding it in dry gusts.

"I suppose you would like an escort out of here?" said Madam Root.

"Please and thank you, ma'am," answered Tinn.

Tinn felt himself go weightless as the stones enveloped him. The sensation was pleasant and cool compared to the inferno he had experienced as a serpent, and he found himself more than happy to simply drift while the kobolds carried him gently upward. He would be free of the cavern by the time the great serpent completed its task.

There would be no more cavern at all by the time the colossus slid down through the layers of stone once more and settled back to its warm slumber. The world could continue to grow and change without it for another eon—and perhaps that was not such a bad thing after all.

THIRTY

KULL WAS MAKING HIMSELF SICK WITH WORRY. He had already *been* sick once, over the edge of the dirigible's basket. Granted, that had been at least partly because the patchwork airship was rocking wildly in the wind, wreaking havoc on Kull's sensitive stomach—but all the worrying definitely wasn't helping. He took a deep breath of salty air and watched the waves drift beneath him, thirty feet below.

It was bad enough Chief Nudd had vanished, but now Tinn? Cole was gone, too, and the boys' mother, and it was all Kull's fault. He knew it was. He had let Tinn copy that map with the forbidden island on it, and now the entire

Burton family was missing. None of them had come home in over a day.

He had already played out dozens of scenarios in his mind, and in nearly all of them the boys were dead, dashed to pieces on the rocks or drowned in the chilly ocean—but in at least one he had considered them marooned on the island without hope of rescue. They could shout and yell and wave their arms, and not a single passing ship would notice them, thanks to the goblin magic. The chief had made it abundantly clear that that island was forbidden, but Nudd was nowhere to be found, and if there was even the tiniest chance the boys might be alive and stranded, Kull had to check.

He had made his way to the docks on the edge of Hollowcliff around midday, nervous that one of the sentries might ask him what he was doing. When the ground started shaking and then the southwest tunnel caved in, Kull had taken advantage of the temporary chaos to untether one of the horde's only airworthy dirigibles and set off into the sky.

He had already been airborne for about an hour when the island finally crept into view. The dirigible's engine purred happily as he stoked it with another heaping scoop of coal. He pressed the wide lever in the center of the steering column to drop the vessel lower, and the pulleys above him creaked and jangled in reply. The airship dipped. Waves crashed against a ring of rocks that circled a seemingly empty patch of blue. A voice drifted toward him on the wind. It was probably nothing—the lapping of the tides—but Kull could not fight back the hope that he would cross that threshold at any moment to find two grateful boys awaiting his rescue. He would scoop them up and fly them safely home, and everything would be all right.

His heart pounded as the dirigible coasted closer to the invisible island. The scene before him blurred, and in another few seconds he was through the magical barrier. The Island of Bones stretched out beneath him, and on it . . .

Kull blinked. He rubbed his eyes.

The Island of Bones—the forbidden isle, the barren wasteland hidden off the coast, impossible to reach except *by* goblins and yet off-limits *to* goblins—was full.

A hundred assorted creatures milled about on the hilly surface. Hobs and trolls and gnomes shuffled their feet, casually taking in the salty breeze, barely even glancing Kull's way as the dirigible floated over their heads. Kull's mouth hung open. Among the shuffling masses, Kull could have sworn he saw Chief Nudd himself sitting on a clump of soil and gazing off into the distance.

"Kull!" cried a voice from the surface. It took a moment to find the source in the crowd, but soon Kull spotted Cole and Fable and Evie, all waving at him. He brought the basket down carefully beside them and tossed the anchor rope around the broken axle of an old cart.

"Otch! Ya wee mad dafties!" he said, climbing out of the basket. "What in the name o' Gogg's Green Garden have ya done now?"

Cole swallowed. His eyes were rimmed with red and his expression looked haunted.

"Kind of a lot," said Fable.

"Aye—I can see that." Kull shook his head. "How did all of ya even *get* here?"

"The same way everything else got here," said Evie. "This island is a garbage dump. So I asked the garbage collectors very nicely if they would give us a ride. They knew the way."

"It's true," said Fable. "The whole island is garbage, all the way down. It's a cavern's worth of digging waste. The delvers had to put it somewhere, so they just kept shoving it up into the ocean until it made its own island. Garbage Island."

"Huh," said Kull. "Isle o' Bones still has a better ring to it." He turned toward the crowd of placid faces occupying the heap. "So, all these folks—these are . . . garbage collectors?"

"No, silly," said Fable. "The garbage collectors are enormous hairy beasts as big as a house. Obviously."

"Right. Obviously," said Kull.

"They're all done being garbage collectors after this, though," said Evie. "I think they're gonna try to remember how to be themselves again."

"I'm just glad they dumped us on top of the heap instead of stuffing us somewhere in the middle," said Cole.

Kull shook his head. "Well, I dinna ken what sorta mischief you an' that brother o' yours cooked up ta land yerselves in this ripe mess, but you had me worried right off my noggin. Glad yer okay, though. Where is Tinn?"

Evie and Fable both turned soberly to Cole. His head hung to his chest. "He . . . he didn't make it out."

Kull pursed his lips. "Did some fool heroic thing again, didn't he?"

Cole nodded.

"Course he did." Kull grunted. "Daft blighted idjit. Any chance he's still . . ."

"I don't know," said Cole.

"Not knowin'. That's somethin'," Kull said with a bracing sniff. "At least I got one o' ya back. That's not nothin' neither."

"You mean *me*?" said Cole.

Kull scowled at him. "Course *you*. Think I meant the

wee witchy?" He shook his head. "Otch. Try ta sell a boy ta the fairies *one time* and the blighter acts like yer na fond of him. Yer brother's right special, lad, but I'd still give my right toe fer ya. Well, I'd give somebody's right toe. And a left one ta go with it." He rubbed his hands on his trousers and took a deep breath. "Well? Come on, then. Let's start gettin' everybody back on solid ground."

Annie Burton's senses returned gradually to the steady rhythm of hoofbeats and the jostling of carriage wheels. Pieces of memories were drifting back to her like fragments of a pleasant dream as she awoke. There had been a cave, and then there had been some kind of giant animal. A snake? Or something like a guinea pig? Such a strange dream. It was all so foggy, but now the fresh air and the smell of wildflowers were slowly washing the foggy feeling away.

The cart hit a bump, and Annie's shoulder bounced off of a boy sitting beside her. She turned her head to look at him. His freckled cheeks and adorable nose were so familiar. What was his name? She found herself brushing her fingers through his shaggy brown hair.

"Mom?" the boy said, eyes widening. "Mom, are you back?"

Mom. Yes. She was *Mom.* And this was *Cole.* How could she have forgotten Cole? Wait. Why were they in a carriage? Hadn't they just been on an island? She could remember the smell of salt water and the lapping of waves against a shore. Had the island been before or after the cave? Her head hurt. The horses clopped and wheels rumbled along packed dirt roads as she tried to sort it all out.

"Annie?" said a low voice.

Annie turned her head. On the other side of her sat a tall, broad-shouldered man. He was handsome in his way, she supposed, but he was also a ragged mess. His clothes were more dirt than fabric, and his beard was long and scruffy. Annie's heart was suddenly pounding. Was this fear? No. This didn't feel like fear. This was something else. It made her whole chest hurt.

She lifted a hand ever so slowly and traced a finger along the man's jaw. She knew this face. It was different, older, but she knew it.

As if on their own, Annie's arms reached up and slid behind the man's neck, and she found herself pulling him closer. Tenderly, the man cupped Annie's head in his broad hands and pressed his forehead against hers. Their noses brushed ever so faintly, and Annie's vision went completely blurry. She breathed in shallow gulps and blinked as hot tears streamed down her face.

"What," she gasped when she could find words again at last, "took you so long?"

Raina listened as her daughter patiently explained, not for the first time, what had happened. It was getting a little easier each time to hold on to the details. "So in the end, the goblins sent word to all the other factions to come and collect their own?" she asked.

"Exactly." Fable nodded. "And some gnomes came to pick up their long-lost gnome friends, and a bunch of trolls came and picked up their long-lost trolls, and so on. And the humans walked along the peninsula to a human town called 'A Butt's Bay' or something, and Cole's dad helped us charter horses and carts back to Endsborough. Oh, and Cole has a dad now."

"None of the forest folk were left behind?"

"Kull and some of the other goblins agreed to stay and shuttle any stragglers back to the forest in their flying balloon things. Candlebeard came out to the island to help, too. He says the hinkypunks will collect as many of those bitter flowers as they can to make a kind of tea that should help everybody sort their brains out again. The ones who got brain-clouded for the longest will probably take a lot longer to set right."

Raina put a hand to her temple to steady her throbbing head. "Good. That's all good. And we are currently . . . ?"

"Riding home with the humans. We're just rolling into Endsborough now."

In another few minutes, Fable was helping Raina out of the carriage. Raina could see one of her daughter's friends helping Annie Burton out of another cart, parked just ahead of theirs. A crowd had already begun massing around them, and the air was abuzz with chatter. A woman in a clean white apron had wrapped her arms around a man in faded, dirty coveralls. She was laughing and crying, and he wasn't saying much at all, but he hugged her back.

It did not take long for the fear and excitement and confusion swirling around the town to find its focus on Fable and Raina.

"That's her," someone hissed in a loud whisper. "Queen of the Deep Dark."

"Pardon me, Your, um, Dark Majesty?"

Raina took a steadying breath and turned her eyes toward a townsperson. It was a broad-chested man in worn trousers and a plaid shirt. He spoke rather timidly for his size.

"Don't mean to offend, but"—he glanced around— "was this . . . you?"

"Was *what* me?" asked Raina.

The man in plaid looked nervous. "All of it?"

"The roads are cracked all over," a woman behind him said. "The old mill's roof collapsed, and I hear there was a sinkhole out by the Warner place so big it swallowed up Jim Warner's barn. A lotta folks were real worried Old Jim went down with the dang thing, on account of they couldn't find him anywhere. We're right glad to see him with you."

"What was that about my barn?" said Old Jim.

"Been a strange one," another voice from the crowd added. "Horses have been spooked all day, and the whole ground feels so hot you could fry an egg on the pavement, but the air is cool as a spring breeze."

"This is another Wild Wood thing, isn't it?" said the original man in plaid. "I thought we were all getting along these days. Did we do something wrong?"

"Did you do something *wrong*?" said Raina. "I don't know. Probably. You usually do."

"The Wild Wood didn't do this!" Fable said, climbing up on the step of the carriage to address the crowd. "They're just as confused by it as you are. But you can all stop worrying. It's over now."

"Stop worrying?" a woman answered. "There's a crevice running through our hayfield makes it look like somebody

294

snapped it in two like a cracker! Goes so deep, I'm not too keen to climb down to see if it even has a bottom!"

"Back up now," Old Jim said. "Was it my *whole* barn?"

"Okay, so there might still be a few things to worry about while we put the town and the forest back together," said Fable. "But everybody is safe now, and that's the important bit."

"We just have to take your word for it?" asked a man toward the middle of the crowd. "I don't much like sitting around and waiting for the next big disaster. I work down in those mines. Know a lot of guys who refuse to go back tomorrow. We just want to watch our own backs. Is there anything we can *do*?"

"Well, actually," said Fable, "there is one thing you could do."

That afternoon, Madam Root heard the clattering of the kobolds rolling pebbles through the passages as they played. A tinkling chime in the mix caught her ear, and she glanced down. One of the bristly creatures held a polished silver coin in its tiny hands. It squeaked triumphantly. At its feet were a handful of rough gemstones.

Madam Root blinked. "Where under earth did you find those?"

Before the kobold could answer, the echoes reached her ears. They were the voices of men, miners setting foot tentatively into the tunnels above her—no doubt surveying the extent of the damage since the great serpent went back into hibernation. The humans were speaking with the hushed, reverent tones of nervous sinners in a church. Madam Root strained her ears.

". . . and she dresses all in gray. Some people say she's a spirit. You'll never see her properly, but she's always watching. I heard she helps miners find their way when their lamps go dark."

"I heard she can walk through solid stone," came another voice.

"I heard she can turn herself into a cave bat," said a third.

"I heard if she kisses you, you can see in the dark."

"I heard it all," agreed the first voice. "And y'all better believe it, every word. Know one thing for certain, long as I'm working these tunnels, you'd best not let me catch you disrespecting our Lady of the Mountain."

Madam Root smiled. For many months after, her kobolds would dance giddily in piles of shiny coins and polished stones and even the occasional ham sandwiches that awaited them reliably in the tunnels each night.

The Echo Point Mining Company, in turn, although it had never produced anything in the way of precious metals, would tap into an unexpected silver vein that season and turn out more profit in a single month than the entire operation had seen in the past decade.

THIRTY-ONE

"THAT'S THE LAST O' THE BLIGHTERS," KULL SAID as Candlebeard helped the addled hob out of his airship. "You'll get her sorted before ya turn her out into the woods?"

Candlebeard nodded and led the wobbling hob away by the elbow.

"Grand," said Kull.

He was alone in the clearing now. Kull knew this stretch of the Wild Wood better than he knew his own horde. He had spent thirteen years crossing through this field on his way to check in on Cole and Tinn. He took a deep breath.

In another few minutes he had prepared the little engine in the dirigible and was just getting ready to untie the anchor ropes when he heard footsteps in the underbrush behind him.

"Oi! Yer na sneakin' up on me," he called out. "Might as well show yourself, ya fat-footed gobby!"

"Sorry," said a voice that made Kull's insides spin in circles. "My lesson on sneaking got canceled." Tinn plodded out of the bushes with slow, labored steps. He was holding one arm against his chest. His face was scratched and bruised and he looked sunburned all over.

Kull made a noise like a lizard choking on a pinecone.

"Are you . . . are you crying?"

"Of course I'm na cryin', ya daft numpty!" Kull wiped snot and tears away from his face with the back of his arm. "Allergic ta havin' my heart smashed all ta bits, thass all. Otch! Come here, my boy!"

Kull was not a hugger. Goblins in general tended to express fond emotions in more concussive ways—and occasionally with biting—but because it had mattered to Tinn, he had agreed to practice.

"That was your best one yet," Tinn told him when the goblin finally let go.

Kull coughed and waved him away. "Where've ya been? Yer poor family's worried out o' their minds over ya!"

When Kull had properly composed himself, they settled into the airship, and Kull coaxed the engine back to life while Tinn related every piece of his eventful day.

"So then the kobolds let me out up on the surface," finished Tinn. "They didn't drop me off anywhere close to home, but I've done enough hanging out with Fable in the forest to get my bearings pretty quick. And—oh, man— fresh air never tasted so good, so I'm not complaining."

Kull shook his head, astonished. "I'll let Chief Nudd know the horde's in debt to the Lady o' the Mountain an' her wee beasties."

"Whoa." Tinn glanced out over the Wild Wood as it glided slowly beneath them. "There's huge holes all over the forest. That one down there's practically a valley. It's going to take Fable and her mom forever to get things back to the way they were before."

Kull snorted. "Why would they waste their time with that?" Tinn looked at him. "Things dinna ever go back ta the way they were. Thass na how life works. Things change. It's what they do. It's like a great big Turas Bàis. Old forest had ta die so a new one could live. Still the same forest. Maybe different will be better—eventually. Give it time."

A few minutes later, Kull set the balloon down near the boys' favorite climbing tree and walked with Tinn up the winding path. It felt profoundly strange to set foot so openly in human territory—but Tinn was still unsteady on his tired legs, and Kull was not about to send him limping home unattended. He stopped when they reached the front walk.

Through the big living room window, they could see Tinn's mother sitting on the brown sofa with her back to the window. Cole was in the armchair across from her, waving his hands as he spoke. By the look of it, he was regaling her with their underground adventures. It appeared to be a good story.

Joseph Burton emerged from the kitchen. Even from outside, Tinn could see that his hair looked clean, his face had been freshly shaved, and he was wearing one of his old shirts from the cedar chest in the attic. He looked even more like Cole. He was carrying three steaming mugs, two of which he passed to Cole and Annie.

"That would be hot chocolate," said Tinn. "They look happy together."

Kull chewed on his lip. If not for the old goblin's meddling all those years ago, the scene in front of them might have been that poor family's every day for the past thirteen years. Without his meddling, Tinn would have never been a part of it at all.

"Aye. They do look happy," Kull said. "Is that . . . good?"

Tinn nodded. "Yeah," he said. "That's good. I kinda thought I would feel more jealous about Cole getting his dad back. He wanted it so bad, and I was just worried about what it meant for me. But this"—he watched as Cole and Joseph clinked hot chocolate mugs—"this is nice, I think. Like maybe Cole is going to be okay without me."

Kull's eyebrows shot up on his wrinkled forehead. "He likely to be without ya any time soon?"

"I don't know," said Tinn. "It's always just been me and Cole. But I hear things don't ever go back to the way they were."

Annie Burton turned her head slowly toward the window, and Tinn saw the melancholy in her eyes. He waved, weakly, and she started when she saw him. For a silent moment, her eyes just widened, and then she was off the couch and rushing for the door.

Tinn glanced down to say goodbye, but by the time the front door flew open, Kull was already gone. The azalea bush on the edge of the property rustled and fell still.

The next few minutes were a whirlwind of hugs and fussing and questions—and Tinn found himself more or less carried back over the threshold. Vaseline and iodine and bandages and ice packs were applied in rapid succession, and by the time Tinn had a moment to himself, he felt almost more exhausted than he had been when he was slogging home through the forest. But he was home.

Cole held the door for his father as Joseph Burton stepped out onto his back porch for the first time in thirteen years. Joseph sniffed in deeply and breathed out a happy sigh. "Look at that garden. You were probably too young to remember a great big bramble that used to come right up to the back of the house. Your mom and I spent hours fighting that thing."

"I remember the bramble," said Cole.

"Oops. Your shoe's untied, kid. Want me to help you with that?"

"I can tie my own shoe," said Cole.

"Yeah. I mean. Of course you can tie your shoes." He rocked on his heels as Cole sat down on the step to fix his laces. "Oh, hey. I can still teach you how to tie a necktie, though. Never know when you might need to dress up fancy for a special occasion."

"Oh," said Cole. "Mom already showed us how to tie a tie. For a dance. At school. Tinn's always come out crooked, but I got mine down pretty good."

"Ah. Right. Good. That's good. You boys had your first dance, then, too? That's great. Great."

"Yeah."

They were quiet. Joseph leaned on the porch railing.

"Are you okay, Dad?"

"Mm? Why wouldn't I be okay? I'm home. I've got my

303

wife and my healthy son—my *sons*. Both of them, because I have *two*. See? I'm even starting to remember things for longer. I'm great."

Cole watched the way his father's eyes crinkled and the way the dimples on his cheeks framed his broad grin. The man had shaved off his scruffy beard with the razor that Annie had kept tucked away in the back of the linen cupboard even after all this time. He looked ten years younger than the ragged man they had found in the tunnels. "I like your face without the beard," Cole said aloud.

"Yeah?" Joseph rubbed his cheeks. "Well, thanks. I like your face, too, kid. Although—you'll be needing to start shaving *your* beard any minute now. Don't think I don't see those whiskers starting to come in." His smile sagged for a moment. "You've probably already learned how to shave?"

Cole shook his head. "Nope. Not yet."

"Well then." Joseph's eyes sparkled and he sat down beside his son. "Maybe there's still a few things I can show you."

"Yeah." Cole leaned in, and Joseph put an arm around his shoulder. "I'd like that."

They listened to the crickets chirp and the wind rustle the willow tree.

THIRTY-TWO

ANNIE BURTON SIGHED CONTENTEDLY AS SHE watched through the window. She sipped her tea, feeling the hot steam on her face. On her own, with two trouble-making boys underfoot, it had been a very long time since Annie had finished an entire cup of tea before it went cold. She was thoroughly looking forward to the experience.

Tinn was in the living room petting Chuffy. That cat had known the boys their entire lives. She had cuts in both of her felted ears and didn't see as well as she used to—but she still always managed to find the one person in the house who most needed to be petting her. She purred mer-rily in Tinn's lap, but his eyes were miles away.

"Hey, big guy," said Annie. "How come you're not out back with your brother and your dad?"

"I thought I'd let them have a little time to themselves," said Tinn.

Annie nodded. She sat down next to him on the comfy brown sofa. "You don't have to do that, you know."

"Do what?"

"Run away from him. He's a good man."

"I know. He seems nice. He and Cole just need each other right now, I think."

"He wants to be *your* dad, too."

"Yeah. He told me that. It's good to hear."

"But . . . ?"

"But . . . I already have a dad. Kull's my dad."

Annie nodded. She peered into the steam rising from her cup for a minute before speaking again. "A long time ago I thought I had just *one* son," she said.

Tinn looked up at her.

"But then it turned out I had *two*. And do you know what I learned once I accepted that I had two sons?"

"That one of those sons was a goblin?"

"That when I allowed myself to love *both* of my sons, I wound up with twice as much love to go around. I didn't have any *less* of one son just because I had *more* of

306

another. It's funny how that works, isn't it? Know what else I learned?"

"That you loved your changeling son a teensy bit more after all because he didn't break that vase your aunt gave you?"

"I learned that I *could* have just as much love for both of you, but I *couldn't* love you exactly the same way—because even if you looked identical down to the last freckle, you were different. You needed a slightly different love from me than Cole did. And that's okay. You can love two people in two totally different ways."

"You're saying I could have two dads," said Tinn. "A goblin dad *and* a human dad."

Annie sipped her tea. "Why not? Who wrote the rules about how many dads a person can have? Up until last year you didn't have any dads at all. Maybe the universe is trying to make it up to you. If you're not careful, we'll have a dozen dads running around this place."

Tinn allowed himself a half smile.

"Look, kiddo. It's okay to let him and Cole have their own time," Annie said. "But give him a chance, huh? No running away."

Tinn nodded. "There's something else I've been meaning to talk to you about."

"Uh-oh. Were you the culprit behind Auntie Shawna's vase after all?"

"No. Not that. That was definitely Cole. It's just . . . I'm realizing more and more that there's a whole big world out there that I'm a part of. That used to scare me, but now . . . I mean, I'll *always* be a part of this world, too, but I've been thinking . . ."

"You want to go on a Turas, don't you?"

"I—what? How do *you* know about a Turas?"

"Chief Nudd spoke to me about it a few months ago." She took a sip of tea.

"A few *months* ago? *I* only got to learn about it a couple *weeks* ago!"

Chuffy, offended by the outburst, slunk down from Tinn's lap and plodded off into the kitchen.

"Well?" said Tinn. "What do you think about it?"

Annie stared deep into her tea. "Lots of cultures have something like it, I suppose. Good to have milestones. Nudd said that there's no specific age for a Turas, though. It's not about turning fifteen or eighteen or twenty."

"It's about the time being right and the goblin being ready," said Tinn.

Annie pursed her lips. "And what if your poor *mom's* not ready?"

Tinn shrugged and looked down at his feet.

"I suppose it doesn't hurt to start thinking about it," she said. "How soon did you have in mind?"

"I was thinking maybe at the end of the school year."

"That's next month!" said Annie. "No, sweetie, that's too soon. I only just got my boys all together again. I thought you meant in a few years. Maybe after you graduate—before you go to college."

"But what if the right time is . . . sooner than that?"

She pursed her lips, and her eyes looked anguished.

Tinn's shoulders sagged. "You're right. Never mind. It was stupid."

Annie's brow furrowed. "Not stupid. Just . . . too soon."

"I understand." Tinn pushed himself up. "I'm really tired. I think I'm gonna just go to bed."

Annie nodded and kissed him on the forehead. "I'll come tuck you in soon."

Tinn closed the door and lay down in his bed. In the dark, he listened to the sound of Joseph Burton's voice as it drifted through the walls. He was singing a muffled lullaby about brothers.

Tinn turned his head. Cole's bed lay empty, aside from the cat, who had curled up on the pillow to nap. The sheets were rumpled where Cole had left them. That morning already felt like a million years ago.

Outside, the lullaby ended, and Tinn could hear the

clunk of the back door and the soft cadence of his mother's voice. Cole said something, and all three of them laughed. Tinn lay in the dark, alone, staring at the faded wallpaper.

Maybe it was the moonlight filtering in through the curtains, but the whole room felt smaller than he remembered—like a comfy sweater that just didn't fit right anymore, no matter how much he squirmed.

The shadows shifted, and Tinn glanced up at the window. A bundle of light, like a fist-sized cluster of fireflies all stuck together, was wobbling on the sill outside the glass.

Curious, he stood up and crept across the room. The bundle of light seemed to notice his movement. It froze.

Tinn knelt down and stared at it through the glass. Up close, the light looked like a dozen paper-thin cobwebs, all glowing brilliant white and shifting around one another, quavering like tissue in the faint night breeze.

"What *are* you?" Tinn whispered aloud.

DIFFERENT, answered a familiar voice. The glow intensified, and Tinn stumbled backward onto the floor of his bedroom.

The light quivered and dimmed.

Nervously, Tinn stood and opened the window. He put out his hand and the Thing scampered onto his outstretched palm. Tinn felt warmth flooding through him—the aches and stings of the day ebbed, and even the burn on Tinn's arm stopped throbbing from within its bandage.

"Whoa," he breathed.

The Thing made a frustrated noise. THEY DO NOT OBEY LIKE THE SHADOWS DID, it moaned. I HAVE BEEN UNABLE TO CONSUME PREY ALL DAY. I HAVE TRIED. WATCH.

In a glimmering blur, it bounded onto Cole's bed. Chuffy's whiskers twitched and she opened one sleepy eye just as the Thing's light swept around her like gossamer ribbons. There was a hiss and a scuffle, and then the cat sprang free and bounded under the chair in the corner— rather more nimbly than Tinn had seen her move in a long time. Her felted ears, he couldn't help but notice, were suddenly free of the cuts and nicks she had earned over the years.

SEE, said the Thing, miserably.

"Did you just try to *eat* my cat?" Tinn said. "Not okay!"

SHE IS BETTER FOR IT.

"That's not the point!" Tinn lowered his voice. "Look, I get that you're confused, but you *cannot* stay here!"

BUT I NEED YOUR HELP, the Thing groaned. I DO NOT KNOW HOW TO BE WHAT I AM BECOMING.

Tinn stared at the sad pile of light. "Yeah? Me neither." The glowing wisps bent and twirled around the Thing as it sank wretchedly into the quilt. "I'm sorry—but I have no idea how to put you back the way you were."

I DO NOT WISH TO GO BACK.

Tinn hesitated. "Why *did* you come here?"

I NEED YOU TO SHOW ME HOW TO DO IT.

"Do what?"

BELONG.

Tinn glanced at the door and then back at the Thing.

"I'm really not the expert you're hoping I am. And I mean it. You really can't stay here."

The Thing was silent. Its glow dimmed, and through the gossamer sheets of light, Tinn could see the creature underneath shivering.

"There's nobody else," Tinn said, "is there?"

The light pulsed feebly.

Tinn sighed and sat down beside the pathetic creature. "I'm sorry. I don't know where you fit in," said Tinn. "I'm not even sure where I fit in anymore." He took a deep breath. "But maybe . . ."

The glow brightened a fraction.

"Maybe the time is right for us to help each other figure it out."

ACKNOWLEDGMENTS

The Oddmire series would not exist without my own goblin boys and all the joy and trouble they bring with them—nor would it exist without their mother, Kat, a force of nature.

I am also grateful to all the teachers who encouraged me and helped me find my voice when I was younger, and to all the skilled educators out there, finding new ways every day to help kids navigate their own strange and winding paths.

And thank you to my fantastic readers for coming along on this journey. Keep reading! I hope you find many more adventures to come—and that you make a few of your own along the way.

THE WILD WOOD

PIXIE RING

THE CABIN

THE BURTONS'

ENDSBOROUGH

OLD JIM'S

ECHO POINT MINE